018

MURDER ON LONDON UNDERGROUND

Peter Hamilton, London Underground's managing director, is horrified when his ex-wife is pushed under a train. Following the murder of a second commuter, he receives an anonymous phone call from an organization calling itself Vortex that is dedicated to preventing the privatization of the network: 'You were the intended victim . . . Next time you won't be so lucky.' Hamilton turns for help to Lyle Revel and Hermione Bradbury, a glamourous couple with a talent for solving murders. But as the death toll rises, the terrorists release a runaway train on the network . . .

JARED CADE

MURDER ON LONDON UNDERGROUND

Complete and Unabridged

LINFORD
Leicester

First published in Great Britain

First Linford Edition
published 2018

A catalogue record for this book is available
from the British Library.

ISBN 978–1–4448–3635–6

Published by
F. A. Thorpe (Publishing)
Anstey, Leicestershire

Set by Words & Graphics Ltd.
Anstey, Leicestershire
Printed and bound in Great Britain by
T. J. International Ltd., Padstow, Cornwall

This book is printed on acid-free paper

1

On the last evening of her life, Fenella Lloyd left the Natural History Museum with a spring in her step and a smile on her face. Work colleagues who saw her one final time knew instinctively that she was happy with her lot in life.

It was just on five-thirty as she entered South Kensington Tube Station. Travelling to work and back home each day in the musty railway tunnels beneath the streets of London was a way of life for her and millions of other commuters. The stations were often dangerously overcrowded, but there could be no denying the Underground network provided the city with its heartbeat.

From inside Fenella's bag the sound of her ringing mobile drew her attention. One look at the caller ID made her stomach muscles tense. Peter's phone calls were becoming more frequent. Perhaps their marriage might have fared better if she had encouraged him to go on an anger management course. Was it cowardice that prompted her to switch off her mobile and thrust it back into her bag? She knew her ex-husband would only become angry if she told him she was on her way to meet her boyfriend Adrian, and she had no intention of spoiling her night by telling him.

At the age of forty, Fenella had fallen in love with a man ten years younger than herself. They had been going out with each other for six months, and she was convinced Adrian was the right man for her. Not only was he blessed with an even temper, but being with him made her feel safe, comforted and loved. Adrian made his living by selling books from his shop in Cyril Court just off the Charing Cross Road. They were planning to have dinner at a restaurant near Tottenham Court Road Tube Station and later see a movie at the Odeon Cinema.

The eastbound Piccadilly line train arrived alongside the platform, and Fenella boarded it. The train became even more crowded as it stopped to disgorge and pick up passengers at stations further along the line. By the time she reached Leicester Square Tube Station, she had decided she would ask her mobile network to block Peter's calls. Her ex-husband needed to stop obsessing about her and get on with his life.

The doors of the train opened with a whooshing sound. Fenella was glad to escape from the throng of humanity inside the overheated carriage. A man with a sharp elbow jostled her as she followed the signs to the northbound Northern Line platform. The platform was almost as crowded as the one she had left behind. She stood near the end of the platform and glanced over the edge. Anyone who fell onto the rails would be instantly electrocuted to death.

From deep inside the tunnel, the rumble of an approaching train increased like a maelstrom as it displaced the dry, fetid air in its path. A familiar electronic voice blared over the tannoy system: 'The next train to arrive on this platform will be a northbound Northern Line train calling at Tottenham Court Road, Warren

Street, Euston, Mornington Crescent, Camden Town and all stations to Edgware — '

Seconds before the train roared out of the tunnel, Fenella felt someone push her from behind. The last sound she heard above her own terrified scream was the wail of the train's horn warning of impending danger.

★   ★   ★

'It's been murder looking after Milsham Castle by ourselves. Lyle and I have really struggled without the help of Mr and Mrs Elliott.'

Hermione Bradbury was speaking on the phone and toying impatiently with a lock of her long red hair. The usual serenity of her pre-Raphaelite face was marred by a frown, and the politeness of her cut-glass English accent belied the exasperation she was feeling at having her afternoon interrupted by a phone call from her elderly employer.

The pompous voice of Lord Milsham boomed down the line from his tax haven in Switzerland. 'The Elliotts are vipers of ingratitude,' he said. 'When they expressed boredom at working at Milsham Castle and asked me if they could come out here to be with me, I was naturally delighted. No one could have been more accommodating than I was — I even paid their air fares out here. I was expecting them to look after me properly. Not get fed up after a year and insist on returning to England.'

'It was appalling ingratitude on the Elliotts' behalf.' Hermione was unable to resist the opportunity to rub salt into her conceited employer's wounds. 'I wouldn't have stood for it myself.'

Lord Milsham added wrathfully, 'I couldn't believe it when Mr and Mrs Elliott asked me for their old jobs back at Milsham Castle. I wouldn't have countenanced the idea if you hadn't told me you were having trouble with the Brockmans.'

'The Brockmans drove Lyle and me up the wall,' Hermione said. 'They are without doubt the laziest caretakers Milsham Castle has ever had. It's a great feeling to have got rid of them. Mr and Mrs Elliott have settled back into the servants' quarters up at the main house. Everything is now back to normal, thank goodness.'

There's no need to sound so pleased,' Lord Milsham said. 'You wouldn't believe the difficulties I've faced since being abandoned by the Elliotts.'

Hermione decided to curtail the conversation. 'Goodness, is that the time? I shudder to think what this call is costing you.'

The frugal peer cut her off with a sharp rejoinder and promptly rang off.

Hermione's exasperation turned swiftly to pleasure as the back door opened and Lyle Revel entered the kitchen. A green mackintosh hung from his tall, athletic frame and his fair hair was beaded with raindrops. With his high-cheekboned face, good-humoured mouth and cleft chin, he exuded an air of health and vitality. There was a look of triumph on Lyle's face because his visit to the hen house had been entirely successful.

One of the qualities Hermione most admired in Lyle was his optimistic belief that most of life's little uncertainties and emergencies could be sorted out with a minimum of fuss and that everything would pan out all right in the end. The couple lived in Nettlebed, a red-brick half-timbered lodge that owed its name to the carpet of nettles that lay beneath the pine trees by the front gates of Lord Milsham's ancestral home. The climbing roses that rampaged up Nettlebed's façade bloomed generously in summer and autumn; now the leaves hung limp and wet, tapping in the breeze against the lead-paned windows. A cold December drizzle hung over the rhododendrons that bordered the driveway leading to Milsham Castle. Summer was a distant memory that would come around in several months' time, bringing with it hazy sunshine and butterflies that flickered over the flowerbeds.

'You'll never guess who that was on the phone,' Hermione said with a grimace.

'Judging by the expression on your face, I'm sure I could make a good guess,' Lyle said with a ripple of laughter in his tenor voice. 'Did you tell Lord Milsham we've given the Brockmans the use of the South Lodge in lieu of a month's notice?'

7

Hermione shook her head. 'He would be furious if he knew they were getting it rent free for a month.'

'What the old miser doesn't know won't hurt him,' Lyle said lightly. 'I think we've treated Ashley and Julia rather well — considering they're short of cash and need time to find somewhere else to live. I'm still convinced they haven't told us the truth about their past.'

Hermione wondered if Lyle was right. She had never cared very much for the Brockmans. Julia's facile charm and vacillating manner were unable to conceal the fact that she was totally ruled by her self-centred husband Ashley. Hermione hoped it wouldn't be long before the Brockmans found a home and vacated the South Lodge. Her distrust of them was so great she wouldn't be satisfied until they left Milsham Castle for good.

'The Brockmans' past could be entirely blameless,' Hermione said provocatively.

Lyle's brown eyes twinkled at her. 'I'll bet you anything that it isn't. Everyone has a past — including us . . . '

It had been a hectic year for Hermione

and Lyle, because juggling their caretaking duties with their professional interests was never easy. Hermione was an accomplished cellist with the Gosfordshire Symphony Orchestra. For the last six months, Lyle had played the lead in *Dead Reckoning* at Wyndham's Theatre in London. Saturday night's closing party had been enjoyed by everyone involved in the production.

Hermione and Lyle had spent the last two days catching up on chores around Nettlebed. After lunch they had driven ten miles to the cathedral town of Gosford in order to buy a Christmas tree for the living room and some scratch-grains for the chickens. It was rare for them to have a Monday afternoon free to themselves, but Milsham Castle was always closed to the public during the winter months.

The phone call that led to them becoming involved in the London Underground murders came around five-thirty that evening. Hermione was in the kitchen heating a saucepan of soup on the green Aga. She forgot about the list of presents she and Lyle were planning to give to family and friends and took up the ringing phone.

'Hello?'

'Hermione, I hope I haven't caught you at an inconvenient moment . . . '

A considerable amount of time had lapsed since she had spoken to Peter Hamilton, but she immediately recognized the American's soft, well-modulated voice. 'Peter, how are you? It's great to hear your voice.'

'There's an urgent matter I need to discuss with Lyle and you. Would you mind coming up to London tonight?'

'Tonight?' Hermione blurted. 'Is anything the matter?'

'I'll explain when you get here. I've already sent a car to pick you up. It should be with you in an hour.'

Hermione's eyebrows rose. There was an unmistakable edge of desperation in Peter Hamilton's voice, and she wondered what was troubling him. She was aware he had trained as a lawyer and had worked as a legal high-flyer for the New York subway before being poached three years ago to run the London Underground railway network. Normally he was a man who was very much in control of his life. Something must be terribly wrong.

'Lyle and I are only too happy to help in any way we can,' she said quickly. 'What's this all about?'

Peter's relief at her acceptance was so palpable it seemed to pass down the line. 'The chauffeur will be under instructions to bring you directly to me at London Underground headquarters.'

Hermione felt her frustration mounting. 'You're not making much sense.'

'Hermione, this is a very bad line. It's hard to hear you properly. I'll explain everything when you get here. I haven't forgotten the favour Lyle and you once did for my parents.'

The dial tone sounded in Hermione's ear. Feeling somewhat baffled, she went down the hall to the living room where Lyle was decorating the Christmas tree. 'That was Peter Hamilton on the phone,' she said thoughtfully. 'I've never known him to sound so desperate. He wants us both to go up to London Underground headquarters tonight.'

Lyle looked surprised. 'Did he say why?'

'He made it very clear he was frightened someone might be listening into his phone conversation. He also mentioned he hasn't forgotten the favour we once did for his parents.'

They were both silent, recalling the events of four years ago. Peter's parents had been the victims of a burglary that had led to a double murder at their home on Long Island in America. Hermione had drawn Lyle's attention to a clue that had been overlooked by the police, and he had subsequently identified the killer with his usual perspicuity.

Lyle frowned. 'If Peter is mixed up in a crime of some sort, I don't see why he should need our help,' he said.

'Not when he's got the combined strength of the Metropolitan and British Transport Police at his disposal,' Hermione agreed.

'Did you accept his offer?'

Hermione nodded. 'You've got a genius for solving murders,' she said. 'I'm just hoping for Peter's sake that his problem isn't as bad as it sounds. After all the ups and downs we've been through this year, I'm looking forward to a peaceful Christmas . . . '

★ ★ ★

Shortly after seven o'clock, Hermione and Lyle arrived in a chauffeured limousine at the headquarters of London Underground Limited. 55 Broadway was a tall multi-tiered building of grey Portland stone situated above St James's Park Tube Station in central London. As the couple made their way towards the circular reception desk in the art deco foyer, they were intercepted by a young black woman who introduced herself as Peter Hamilton's personal assistant and invited them to accompany her to his office.

A lift took Hermione and Lyle to the ninth floor, where they followed the woman down a long corridor panelled in dark wood. After knocking on a door at the end and receiving a summons from within, she stood aside for them to enter a large office was lit by wall sconces and dominated by a mahogany desk. She then departed, closing the door.

Peter Hamilton was standing by the window in a grey business suit, with his red hair slightly brushing the back of his white collar. He turned and greeted them in a tired voice. His monk-like face was just as Hermione remembered — thin and lean, with a high beaked nose, and intelligent eyes set deep in bony sockets. What shocked her more than anything was his haggard appearance — he looked like a man who hadn't slept or eaten for forty-eight hours.

'Peter, Hermione and I are assuming it must be bad news for you to send for us in this way.'

Peter released a sigh. 'It could hardly get any worse,' he said, gesturing to them to sit down. Despite his obvious fatigue, he remained standing. 'On Friday evening a woman was pushed under a train at Leicester Square Tube Station. There was another fatality this morning at Baker Street. The police have launched a major murder investigation. The first victim was my former wife Fenella Lloyd.'

The couple stared at him in shock. Although they had never known the dead woman, they could see how upset their friend was by his ex-wife's death.

'Oh, my God . . . '

'Peter, we're so sorry . . . '

Peter Hamilton was looking as if he'd been to hell and back. 'Fenella was killed just before six o'clock. It was your typical Friday evening rush hour. Incredibly, no one saw who pushed her in front of the oncoming train. The platform was severely overcrowded. Several commuters claim they saw the suspected killer fleeing from the scene, but none of the descriptions matched up. It's obvious they described the first man they saw afterwards who appeared to be acting suspiciously.'

Lyle said, 'Surely the police must have some leads?'

'The police examined the CCTV footage and came up with nothing. The cameras around the station record on a time-delay sequence. The captured foot-age shows a series of recorded shots from other areas of the station. But there's no actual footage of Fenella's murder — only its aftermath. By the time the police arrived at Leicester Square, the killer had already got away.'

'Hermione and I are prepared to do anything we can to bring Fenella's killer to justice,' Lyle said firmly. 'But we're going to need more to go on. Have you spoken to Fenella's family and friends?'

Peter nodded. 'Everyone who knew Fenella is shocked by the senselessness of her murder. She worked as a palaeontologist at the Natural History Museum. She was well-respected by her work colleagues.'

'Is there anyone special in Fenella's life?'

'Yes — there's a fellow by the name of Adrian Knowles. He owns a book shop in Cyril Court just off the Charing Cross Road. Fenella was planning to have dinner with him on Friday night.'

'Was Adrian Knowles the reason why you got divorced?' Hermione asked intuitively.

Peter winced. 'Fenella and I got divorced six months ago. She met him soon afterwards. Our marriage fell apart because she accused me of being wrapped up in my career. She wanted to have children. I've already got six children from my first marriage and I don't want any more. As much as Fenella and I loved each other, we never seemed to agree on anything.'

'Who was the second victim?' Lyle asked.

Peter heaved a sigh, and the look of distress in his eyes was terrible to behold. 'Oscar Sinclair owned a hairdressing salon in Hammersmith. He was on his way to work during the rush hour this morning. The CCTV footage shows a shot of him appearing on the westbound Hammersmith and City Line platform at Baker Street, and then switches to images from around other areas of the station. Well-meaning commuters have inundated police with descriptions of various people they suspect might be the killer. Again none of them tally. At five o'clock this evening, a man rang me on my work mobile. He told me, 'You were the intended victim at Baker Street. Next time you won't be so lucky.''

The couple stared at him in astonishment. 'Are you saying Oscar Sinclair was mistaken for you?' Lyle said.

Peter nodded. 'I rang the police immediately and told them about the call. They've agreed to offer me round-the-clock protection. I'm supposed to go directly to my home in St John's Wood and wait for the protection team to arrive. But first I wanted to speak to you both.' He broke off abruptly and gazed out of the window.

Hermione felt a slither of apprehension. 'What is it?'

'I'm sorry — for a moment I thought I saw a shadow on the fire escape.' Peter's shoulders relaxed visibly. 'There's no one there. It's probably just another pigeon roosting down for the night. There's something I want to tell you both,' he added anxiously. 'But I'd rather not do it here just in case my office is bugged. My chauffeur is waiting downstairs to take us to Claridge's Hotel. It will be safer to continue our conversation there.'

2

As the doors closed and the lift began descending towards the lobby, Lyle said with a glimmer of frustration in his eyes, 'The odds of finding the killer don't look good.'

'Unless this madman is seen on CCTV committing another murder,' Hermione said, 'he may never be caught and arrested.'

Peter Hamilton's response left them feeling deflated. 'London Underground has 270 stations. An average of four million passengers' journeys are recorded on the network each day.'

Hermione exchanged glances with Lyle. How on earth were they supposed to expose the killer when the odds were so heavily stacked against them? It seemed their friend was setting them an impossible task.

Lyle said, 'Peter, can you describe the voice of the person on the phone who claimed you were the intended victim?'

'The caller spoke in a low, guttural voice.'

'Has it occurred to you that a member of the public wouldn't have access to your work mobile number?'

Peter nodded. 'London Underground employs twenty thousand people. Any one of them could have phoned our directory inquiries team and obtained my mobile number without arousing suspicion. My appointment as managing director of London Underground is bound to have scuppered a few people's ambitions, especially since I'm an American.'

Hermione said, 'Who was the most likely contender for your job?'

'Daniel Fitzpatrick, my deputy managing director.'

'How long has he worked for the company?' Lyle asked.

'Over thirty years. He started off as a train driver and worked his way up the LUL ladder. His reputation for being ferociously ambitious is well-deserved.'

The lift stopped at the fourth floor, the doors opened, and a man in a business suit stepped inside. Beneath his iron-grey hair there was a strong touch of colour in his lean face with its sharp, jutting cheekbones and strong chin. There was a look of keen intelligence in his eyes that conveyed the impression he did not suffer fools lightly.

'Peter, I've been trying to get hold of you,' he said, speaking in the smooth, unctuous manner of a professional raconteur.

Peter's response was guarded. 'Daniel, these are my friends. You can speak freely in front of them.'

Hermione's pulse quickened. So this was Daniel Fitzpatrick . . . Her father was a member of the Tory cabinet, and Daniel Fitzpatrick reminded her of one of her father's more ruthless political adversaries.

The doors closed and the lift began descending once again.

Daniel Fitzpatrick said, 'Two officers from the police protection team are waiting downstairs in the lobby for you. It's taken the Met longer to organize a team than they hoped. Several officers were on holiday and had to be recalled for duty.'

'The police have certainly taken their time to get here,' Peter remarked with a hint of sarcasm.

'It's imperative you take this threat against your life seriously and follow any instructions the police give you. London Underground can function without you while you're on bereavement leave.'

'How many times do I have to tell you?' Peter snapped. 'I'm not going on bereavement leave. Doing nothing for the next two weeks will drive me around the bend. If anyone is going to bump me off, I'd rather they do it here at 55 Broadway. With any luck, one of our CCTV cameras might even capture the event for prosperity.'

Unfazed by the other's outburst, Fitzpatrick said firmly, 'Peter, it's for your own good. I've spoken to the board of LUL, and this is our joint decision in the matter.'

Peter's voice was loaded with sarcasm. 'And who's going to run LUL in my absence?'

'The board has asked me to act as spokesperson.'

The tension in the lift was so palpable that Hermione and Lyle were glad when they reached the lobby. Once outside the lift, Peter turned and faced his deputy.

'I tried to get hold of you in your office on Friday evening just before six o'clock,' he said ingratiatingly. 'Where were you?'

Fitzpatrick smiled regretfully. 'I had an emergency dental appointment. Of all the rotten luck.'

Peter kept his tone casual. 'Your answer service picked up again when I rang you this morning.'

'Was it important?' Fitzpatrick's piercing gaze pressed him for an answer.

Peter produced an affable smile. 'LUL's press office called. I forget what it was about.'

'Leave it to me, Peter. I'll be in touch.'

Unimpressed by his deputy's assurances, Peter introduced himself to the two police officers who were waiting for him in the lobby; they were part of an eight-man team that had been assigned to protect him.

Daniel Fitzpatrick pressed a button inside the lift. Hermione looked at him and was unable to rid herself of an impression of a wolf in sheep's clothing. Before the lift doors closed and he disappeared from sight, he gave Peter's retreating back such a look of extraordinary malevolence that Hermione almost exclaimed aloud in astonishment. It occurred to her that if Daniel Fitzpatrick was responsible for the two Tube murders, he would almost certainly make another attempt on his rival's life before long.

Uncertain if she had been gazing at the face of a murderer, Hermione followed Lyle and Peter Hamilton outside to where the latter's limousine was parked by the kerb.

★   ★   ★

On the journey to Claridge's Hotel, silver javelins of rain struck against the limousine windows, then slid down the glass like teardrops. Peter Hamilton's face was swallowed up in shadows, but there could be no mistaking the tension in his voice when he said, 'I've never liked Daniel Fitzpatrick. His obsequious manner grates on my nerves like a file on glass.'

'Peter, your attitude towards him just now was distinctly antagonistic,' Lyle warned him.

'Daniel Fitzpatrick is after my job,' Peter said grimly. 'His motive for killing Fenella could be to convince others that I'm not fit to run London Underground. He obviously mistook Oscar Sinclair for me when he pushed him under the train at Baker Street.'

Hermione wished she could find a way to ease Peter's distress. But what do you say to a man whose ex-wife has been brutally murdered and who had the torment of knowing someone else had mistakenly been murdered in his place? Lyle's masculine and reassuring presence took the edge off her nerves, and she felt safer for knowing two police protection officers were following close behind them in a marked police car.

It had stopped raining by the time the limousine drew up outside Claridge's Hotel. Brook Street was slicked with rain, and the cold night air discouraged Hermione and her companions from lingering on the pavement. The warmth of the chandelier-hung black-and-white-tiled lobby was a welcome respite. The art deco elegance of a bygone era was all around Hermione and Lyle as they followed Peter across the lobby to the lifts. His profile was inscrutable, but there was no doubt in Hermione's and Lyle's mind that their friend was inwardly torn apart with grief over Fenella's murder. Peter pressed the button, and they waited in silence for the lift to descend.

From behind them, a cheerful easy-going voice said, 'Lyle, it's been a long time. How are you?'

Lyle turned and saw a smiling, gaunt-faced Irishman sitting behind the theatre desk near the stairwell. The years had not been kind to thirty-seven-year-old Reggie Dalloway: his brown hair was turning grey and his sallow face was showing definite signs of sagging.

'Reggie, how are you?' Lyle asked.

'Fine, fine. It seems hardly any time has passed since we were on location filming

The Bawdy Adventures of Tom Finnegan.'

Reggie's involvement in the film came as news to Hermione. Lyle had played the supporting role of a lascivious Belgian aristocrat who ravished several maidens in an eighteenth-century British romp that had proven moderately successful at the box office when it was released two years ago.

'I wasn't sure if you'd remember me,' Reggie continued. 'I only had a small part as a peasant who was locked up in the stocks and pelted with rotten eggs.'

'You were wonderful. Everyone I know says so.'

Lyle's flattery came as no surprise to Hermione. He had been in the acting business long enough to know that all actors wanted to be told they were brilliant regardless of whether it was the truth.

Gratified by Lyle's outrageous compliment, Reggie smiled and said, 'You're not the first person to tell me how good I was in my role. I've lost count of the customers I've sent along to Wyndham's

Theatre to see you in *Dead Reckoning*.'

'Saturday night's closing party was huge fun,' Lyle said with an ingratiating smile. 'It's a shame you missed it.'

'It's nearly time for me to close up shop,' Reggie said. 'Would you like to go somewhere for a drink?'

'Reggie, nothing would give me greater pleasure,' Lyle said. 'It's a shame one of the guests staying in the hotel has asked Hermione and me to dinner to discuss a business matter. We can't get out of it as much as we would like to for your sake. How long have you worked here?'

'For the last ten years — that's between acting jobs, of course,' Reggie replied. 'Gala Theatre Tickets, my employer, rents the space from the hotel. Lyle, I can get tickets to any show you want.'

'In that case, I look forward to hearing your recommendations tomorrow morning. Good night, Reggie. It's been good catching up with you.'

The lift arrived and Lyle and his companions stepped inside.

★　★　★

Sighing dispiritedly, Reggie watched the lift doors close and switched off his computer. It was time to don his duffle coat and scarf and go home.

He looked forward to seeing Lyle Revel again on the off-chance that the actor might be able to put him in touch with some contacts that could help kick-start his acting career. He hadn't had a decent acting role in two years. Lyle Revel and Hermione Bradbury were an attractive couple with an indefinable air of glamour about them, and Reggie felt a twinge of envy. There was nothing he would like more than to be accepted into their social circle.

Outside the hotel, Reggie stamped his feet in the bitterly cold air and said good night to the doorman. The prospect of returning to his small flat in Bryanston Street behind Marble Arch Tube Station was an attractive one in this weather. He planned to spend the rest of the night in front of the electric fire learning a speech from Twelfth Night in preparation for an audition he was attending in a couple of days' time.

Reggie walked along Brook Street, then turned right into Davies Street and headed towards West One Shopping Centre. Once inside the building, out of the freezing cold, he hurried past the shoppers and descended the escalator to Bond Street Tube Station.

The westbound Central Line platform was crowded. He suspected, quite rightly, that the line was suffering from one of its interminable delays. Judging by the fancy dress costumes a lot of revellers were wearing, it was obvious they were on their way to Christmas parties. One of Santa Claus's elves grinned wickedly at him and moved on.

Despite its many attractions, London was no substitute for Ireland. Without warning, Reggie found himself feeling homesick for his father's pub in Killarney. There was nothing he enjoyed more than a good banter with the locals. A couple of minutes later, a fight broke out between two women at the far end of the platform. But the noise of the fight was drowned out by the thunder of the approaching train.

Suddenly Reggie Dalloway was given a brutal push from behind that sent him nose-diving off the edge of the platform.

In the terror-crazed seconds before he died, he admitted to himself, after years of denial, that his acting career had been a total failure. He was also aware that, for all its sham and drudgery and broken dreams, it was still a beautiful world — and he would have given anything not to leave it all behind . . .

3

Hermione and Lyle were dining with Peter Hamilton in the elegant suite he had booked for them at Claridge's Hotel. The two police officers assigned to protect their friend were positioned outside in the corridor.

'Assuming for the moment your deputy Daniel Fitzpatrick isn't the killer,' Lyle said thoughtfully, 'what other enemies do you have within the company?'

Having wolfed down his dinner in a remarkably short space of time, Peter poured himself another glass of wine and took his time replying. The colour had returned to his cheeks, and he was in no hurry to return to his house in St John's Wood because it contained too many painful memories of his failed marriage to Fenella.

'The two trade unions who look after the rights of the Tube workers are waging an endless war with London Underground,' he said, allowing a fraction of the anger he was feeling to seep into his voice. 'As usual, they're far from happy with their latest pay rise.'

'Are you referring to the RMT and Tessa unions?' Hermione queried.

'Over the years, the unions have been responsible for numerous strikes on London Underground. Every time they go on strike, the whole Tube network shudders to a halt. Millions of Londoners are faced with the difficulty of getting to work. A single day's strike results in the city losing millions of pounds in lost revenue. During the last twelve months, a violent splinter group of the RMT known as Vortex has broken away from the main party.'

Lyle's interest sharpened. 'Do you think Vortex murdered your ex-wife and Oscar Sinclair?'

'I'm absolutely certain of it,' Peter said. 'Vortex's sole objective is to prevent London Underground and the British government from privatizing the Tube in six months' time. The British government can no longer afford to subsidize the network to the tune of five hundred million pounds each year. Vortex is convinced the private companies who are poised to buy up London Underground will be motivated by profit to reduce staff wages and halve the number of jobs on the network. I probably shouldn't tell you this, but Vortex is right to be paranoid. The private companies aren't to be trusted.'

'The closure of London Underground's ticket offices has resulted in a lot of adverse publicity,' Hermione remarked. 'Presumably it's also been a cause of bitter dispute for the unions?'

'The Oyster Card revolution has led to ninety-eight percent of all our customers buying their tickets online,' Peter said. 'It wasn't financially viable to keep the ticket offices open — not when only two percent of our customers were queuing up to buy their tickets. A year ago, London Underground entered into an agreement with the private companies to shut down all the ticket offices before the network is officially privatized. As you can imagine, this has led to huge job losses and more will follow once London Underground is privatized.'

'It's easy to understand why Vortex is

determined to fight privatization every step of the way,' Lyle remarked. 'What sort of threats have you received?'

'Vortex has rung me on no less than four occasions demanding I call off privatization,' Peter said. 'A different man has spoken to me each time and promised dire consequences if I disobey. As you know, I received a fifth anonymous phone call earlier tonight. 'You were the intended victim at Baker Street. Next time you won't be so lucky.''

The television was playing silently in the background because they had been watching the news coverage of the Tube murders before dinner. Now, as London Underground's iconic roundel appeared on the screen, Lyle grabbed the remote control and turned up the sound. 'Listen to this,' he urged them.

The voice of the newscaster was saying, 'A short while ago, Vortex claimed responsibility for the murder of Oscar Sinclair. The fifty-seven-year-old hair-dresser was on his way to work when a member of the terrorist organization pushed him under a train at Baker Street station during this morning's rush hour. The dead man's grieving wife and mother of their five-year-old twin boys has confided her family is devastated by his murder. Now in a chilling twist, Vortex is claiming Oscar Sinclair was mistaken for London Underground's managing director Peter Hamilton. Vortex also admits to deliberately targeting his ex-wife Fenella Lloyd, who was pushed under a train at Leicester Square on Friday night. The terrorist organization claims it will go on killing innocent members of the public unless London Underground and the British government call off plans to privatize the Tube network . . . '

The trio listened in stunned silence to the rest of the broadcast, then Lyle muted the sound. 'Vortex is clearly prepared to stop at nothing to get their way,' Peter said angrily. 'During the last six months, its members have sabotaged four different signalling systems across the network, making it impossible to run trains on the affected lines until extensive repairs were carried out. There have been a number of trackside fires resulting in the suspension

36

of train services on another seven lines. Our stations have been targeted with hoax phone calls claiming bombs have been planted on the network. Fire alarms have been activated without due cause. There have been numerous station closures while the emergency services investigated each incident. Each time Vortex has claimed responsibility.'

Hermione said, 'Vortex clearly poses a considerable threat to the public.'

'The police have had six months to identify Vortex. So far they haven't come up with a single clue.'

'There's going to be an even bigger public backlash against Vortex and privatization now they've admitted to carrying out the murders,' Lyle said grimly. 'Peter, I hate to say this, but your stance on privatization is going to come under attack from all sorts of people. You've got to prepare yourself and be ready for your critics.'

Peter's voice tightened. 'My task will be a lot easier if you both help me by infiltrating Vortex. It's imperative we find out these terrorists' true identities and expose them for the scum they are.'

Hermione felt a chill of apprehension. 'How do you suppose we do that when we haven't got any clues to go on?' she asked.

'I happen to know for a fact that Vortex's latest anonymous call was made to me from Pembroke Grove Tube Station.'

The couple stared at him in surprise. 'How can you be so sure?' Lyle said.

'I heard a man broadcasting a tannoy message in the background of the call. Customers were being advised that their next eastbound train had left Laburnum Lane and would be with them at Pembroke Grove in two minutes' time. It was clear from the muffled quality of the tannoy message that the call was being made from somewhere inside the station.'

'Vortex's anonymous caller must work at Pembroke Grove,' Hermione said swiftly.

Peter nodded in agreement. 'The sound of the tannoy message suddenly became louder because a door leading off platform two opened with an unmistakable groaning sound, then shut with a loud clunk. I've heard it myself when I've passed through Pembroke Grove on my way to the local radio station in order to be interviewed about LUL matters.'

Hermione said, 'Whoever was speaking to you must have been interrupted by a colleague entering the room where they were making the call.'

'Am I right in thinking you want Hermione and me to go undercover at Pembroke Grove?' Lyle asked.

'That's the big idea,' Peter said with a relieved smile. 'You can both claim to be new recruits to London Underground's graduate trainee scheme. That way your lack of procedural knowledge won't arouse suspicion. Each new trainee is assigned to a station and shadows the staff there to find out as much as possible about the workings of the station in relation to the rest of the network. Your cover couldn't be simpler.'

Hermione turned to Lyle and said, 'I can't see the BBC releasing you from your obligations.'

'What obligations?' Peter asked, frowning.

'I'm under contract to the BBC to take part in their radio thriller season,' Lyle explained. 'Dead Reckoning, the play I've just finished appearing in at Wyndham's Theatre, is being recorded over the next three days at Broadcasting House. My contract with the BBC is iron-clad. They won't let me out of it.'

'That only leaves me to infiltrate Vortex,' Hermione said, looking at Lyle. 'My cover story has a much better chance of being believed than yours, since your face has recently appeared on theatre posters all over the West End.'

'Does that mean you accept my offer?' Peter asked.

Hermione drew a deep breath. 'All right,' she said. 'I'll do it.'

The trio spent another twenty minutes discussing strategies to ensure the success of their plan. After their friend had left, Lyle said anxiously, 'Hermione, are you sure you want to go through with this?'

'I don't see what other choice we've got,' Hermione said. 'Vortex has promised to go on killing innocent members of the public unless the British government and London Underground cancel plans to privatize the Tube . . . '

* * *

Over the next hour, Hermione and Lyle braved the cold and visited Leicester Square and Baker Street Tube Stations. Outside the entrance to each station, members of the public had laid flowers and lit candles in tribute to the two murdered commuters, Fenella Lloyd and Oscar Sinclair.

There was a marked police presence at both stations, and Hermione and Lyle recognized this as a belated initiative on the authorities' part to instil confidence in the public. The platform where each victim had been pushed to their death yielded nothing in the way of physical clues. They were reminded that the best place to lose yourself is in a crowd. It was little wonder Vortex's assassin had been able to disappear after each attack.

The publicity arising from the two murders had not dampened the ardour of thousands of Christmas shoppers who were out in force buying presents for their loved ones. Some people were going so casually about their business as to give rise to the belief that they hadn't heard about the attacks. Judging by the number of revellers and partygoers, it was apparent that for some people nothing was going to get in the way of their enjoyment of the festive season.

Outside Leicester Square Tube Station, a film crew from ITV was filming interviews with members of the public who were expressing their bewilderment and grief at the senselessness of the two murders. It seemed to Hermione and Lyle that words were inadequate at times like this to express the horror and outrage of law-abiding people who'd had their trust shattered in such a brutal way. A volunteer from St Barnaby's Hospice, dressed in a Santa Claus costume, was soliciting donations from the public inside the station ticket hall. Hermione and Lyle dropped some coins into his box in a bid to spread some good cheer. Feeling cold and dispirited, they hailed a taxi and returned to Claridge's.

As the couple were crossing the hotel lobby, they saw two plain-clothes Metropolitan police officers from the Homicide and Serious Crimes Unit standing by the theatre desk. DI Deveril and DS Snare were conferring in low voices with the hotel's security manager.

'I wonder what the hell Deveril is doing here,' Lyle muttered. 'This doesn't bode well.'

'Keep calm and say as little as possible,' Hermione whispered. 'Don't let him provoke you.'

She was aware that DI Deveril hated Lyle's guts, and she knew only too well the reasons why. Long before Lyle had met Hermione and set up home with her at Nettlebed, he'd had a brief, if enjoyable, fling with DI Deveril's ex-girlfriend DS Penny Lane. Ever since that time, DI Deveril had harboured a grudge towards him. It simply wasn't in DI Deveril's nature to let bygones be bygones. Lyle had since upstaged DI Deveril by solving a number of murder cases that the police officer had been assigned to investigate. As a consequence, DI Deveril blamed his lack of promotion within the ranks of the Metropolitan Police Force on Lyle and detested him even more.

The moment DI Deveril saw Lyle, a

look of displeasure sprang up in his eyes. He stepped forward, deliberately blocking Hermione's and Lyle's progress to the lifts. 'Revel, what are you doing here?' he demanded in a harsh baritone voice.

Lyle braced himself for the other's inevitable icy blast of disdain. 'Hermione and I are staying here in the hotel.'

DI Deveril hadn't changed over the years. He still radiated an air of smug superiority and strained at the seams of his suit. A moustache every bit as black as his hair accentuated his overall pasty complexion, while his ruddy cheeks indicated he had not lost his fondness for regular pints of ale. It was hard to imagine him having a private life. He looked like the sort of police officer who was never happy unless he got his man. His next question filled the couple with foreboding.

'Where were you both around eight o'clock tonight?'

'Having dinner in our hotel suite,' Lyle replied.

'Does the name Reggie Dalloway ring any bells?'

'He works here at the theatre desk,'

Lyle said. 'I'm a friend of his. Why do you ask?'

DI Deveril smiled ferociously. 'Reggie Dalloway was pushed under a train at Bond Street Tube Station earlier tonight.'

Lyle was horror-struck. 'What?'

'You can't be serious,' Hermione blurted. 'What happened?'

'Have you any idea who killed him?' DI Deveril demanded.

Lyle's natural sense of caution reasserted itself. 'None at all.'

DI Deveril took a step forward. 'I can do without your interference in this case, Revel. I'm in charge of this investigation, not you. *Comprendez-vous?*'

Lyle slowly exhaled. 'The idea of interfering in this case never crossed my mind,' he said stiffly.

DI Deveril looked far from reassured. Standing behind him was DS Nicholas Snare, a broad-shouldered man with curly brown hair who possessed a solemn-looking face that was capable of breaking unexpectedly into a wolfish grin. At that moment there was nothing in Nicholas Snare's serious manner to indicate that he and Lyle were good friends.

Hermione heard the doors of the lift open behind her. She stepped quickly inside, followed by Lyle. Behind DI Deveril's back, Nicholas Snare gave them both a look of commiseration. Hermione liked Nicholas and hoped it would not be long before she and Lyle saw him again. In the past, the police sergeant had supplied them with inside information that had enabled Lyle to solve several cases that would have gone unsolved if the outcome had been left up to DI Deveril.

After the lift doors closed, Hermione said with a shudder, 'I can't believe Reggie Dalloway is dead. You were only talking to him a few hours ago.'

Lyle was reeling with shock. 'What possible reason could anyone have for killing Reggie? He was such a likeable, harmless sort of fellow.'

'I could make a good guess.' Hermione's throat was swollen with emotion. 'I wish Deveril wasn't in charge of this case. His only talent is for arresting low-life criminals who share the same IQ as him.'

Lyle clenched his jaw. 'Don't I know it!'

Hermione gazed anxiously at him. 'I wonder how many more random members of the public Vortex is going to kill.'

'There was nothing random in Vortex's decision to kill Fenella Lloyd. Being Peter Hamilton's ex-wife signed her death warrant. The only reason Peter Hamilton is still alive is because Oscar Sinclair was mistakenly killed instead. So far, Vortex has been carefully pre-selecting its victims. We're dealing with a group of terrorists — we can't afford to believe everything they say. They've got no respect for the truth or human life. We've got to be on our guard with them.'

'What possible motive could Vortex have for deliberately targeting Reggie?' Hermione asked.

'There's always blackmail.'

Hermione stared at Lyle in surprise. 'Blackmail? What do you mean?'

'Reggie might have witnessed one of the murders and decided to extort money from Vortex in return for his silence. It would have been easy enough for him to follow Vortex's assassin from the scene of the crime.'

'I never met Reggie until tonight, but it sounds highly improbable to me. Do you really think he would have stooped so low?'

'On the other hand,' Lyle said thoughtfully, 'Reggie might have stumbled across the identity of Vortex's assassin by accident. People who stay here are always going to the theatre. It's one of the major attractions of coming to London. Suppose Vortex's assassin came to Reggie?'

'Since when are the members of Vortex able to afford to stay at Claridge's?'

'Sales of theatre tickets aren't restricted to residents of the hotel,' Lyle pointed out. 'It's much more likely Vortex's assassin came in off the street. I can see Reggie processing Vortex's theatre tickets and taking his credit card details.'

'After which, Reggie would have been able to identify the killer and threaten him with exposure unless he paid up,' Hermione concluded. 'If you're right, Reggie must have really believed he'd hit the jackpot when he came face to face with Vortex's assassin. It's too bad he didn't realize just how dangerous it can be to blackmail Vortex.'

Lyle drew a deep breath. 'My inner voice is telling me Vortex bided its time, then followed Reggie to Bond Street Tube Station tonight and gave him a fatal shove under the train. I wonder if Reggie had a girlfriend or wife.'

'Well if he did, I'm afraid she's going to be extremely upset when she hears he's been murdered,' Hermione said with a shiver.

'I just hope for her sake, Hermione, that Reggie didn't tell her what he knew.'

'Meaning she might also try and blackmail Vortex and become their next victim?'

Lyle nodded grimly. 'Reggie could never keep a secret for long. I hope for her sake that if she does know anything, she goes straight to the police.'

4

Hermione and Lyle were watching the morning news. All the television channels were leading with the story of the Tube murders. Photographs of the three victims dominated the bulletins.

Channel Seven's newsreader was saying, 'Early this morning, Vortex claimed responsibility for the murder of Reggie Dalloway, who died under a train at Bond Street Tube Station last night. The terrorist organization is threatening to murder more commuters unless the British government and London Underground back down on their plans to privatize the Tube. Some commuters are now so terrified of traveling on the Tube that they're signing an online petition to boycott privatization . . .'

Hermione pressed a button on the TV remote control that took her to BBC One.

' . . . Vortex's ultimatum has been greeted with an uproar of condemnation from politicians and officials from London Underground. The RMT and Tessa unions have released statements saying they are peacefully opposed to privatization and not in any way affiliated with the violent splinter group known as Vortex . . . '

Hermione switched to Channel Five's news coverage.

' . . . A short while ago the Prime Minister issued a statement from Downing Street condemning Vortex. She denounced the terrorist organization's activities as vile and unlawful, and promised that the forces of law and order would track them down and bring them to justice. We cross live now to Downing Street . . . '

Hermione and Lyle exchanged glances. 'If my parents find out I'm embroiled in another murder case, they'll be furious with you.'

Lyle smiled. 'Your parents are on holiday in Corsica. There's little chance of them finding out what we're up to. They approve of me more than you realize. In fact, they recently told me you were in danger of becoming a shrew before we met and that you needed a strong-willed man like me to tame you.'

Hermione laughed in spite of herself. 'That's just the sort of cheap comment my mother would make. I've got a successful career as a cellist because I've worked hard for it. But she would insist on giving up her career as a painter when she married Daddy in order to support his political career. And now she regrets it. I always vowed I would never give up my musical career for any man.'

'Including me,' Lyle said good-humouredly.

'If you must know,' Hermione added with a self-conscious smile, 'I was in danger of becoming a shrew before you came into my life. I'd made one or two poor decisions romantically. The men I was attracted to didn't fulfill their early promise of artistic genius, so they had to go.'

'Meaning Inglebert the poet whose verses didn't rhyme?' Lyle teased.

'And Duncan the songwriter whose voice sounded like two pieces of burnt toast being rubbed together,' Hermione confirmed ruefully. 'Instead I ended up with Lyle Revel — an actor with a love of the limelight and a talent for solving murders.'

'Our life together certainly isn't dull,' Lyle said, his eyes twinkling.

Hermione conceded he had a point. Being in a relationship was crucial to her well-being, and Lyle had a way of bringing out the best in her. He felt the same way about her, too. She was aware he respected her honesty and independence; she had an excellent head for business and could be relied on to drive a hard bargain, whether she was renting out the grounds of Milsham Castle for a wedding or hiring out the tennis courts. Even so, she knew Lyle was right to be worried about her decision to go uncover at Pembroke Grove Tube Station in a bid to expose Vortex. It involved a considerable amount of risk and possible danger to herself. But her determination to stand by her promise to Peter Hamilton had been reinforced by the morning's news coverage of the three murders.

In response to a knock at their suite, Hermione went to the door. A room service waiter entered with a cardboard box the size of a suitcase bearing her name and the logo of London Underground on it. He then departed with a tip from Lyle.

After unpacking the box, Hermione announced, 'My uniform has arrived on the morning Vortex is the number-one news story across Great Britain.' She gazed ruefully at the shapeless blue blouse and trousers, as well as a parka and a pair of flat-heeled black Doc Martin shoes. 'It's not exactly Versace, is it?'

'It's sure to look better when you're wearing it,' Lyle said in his most hypocritically soothing voice.

Hermione threw him a look of reproach. 'It looks hideous now,' she complained, 'so I don't imagine it will look any better after I've put it on.'

She could see by the amused expression on Lyle's face that he agreed with her. Earlier that morning, Peter Hamilton had phoned the suite and asked her to keep an appointment for nine o'clock at London Underground's training centre, Ashfield House, in West Kensington. She was scheduled to meet a training instructor who was going to provide her with an overview of what it was like working for the company. Later that afternoon she was due to begin her first shift at Pembroke Grove Tube Station. Picking up her uniform, she went into the bedroom to change into it.

The phone rang moments later, and the jovial voice of DS Nicholas Snare of the Metropolitan Police filled Lyle's ear. 'Is that his Highness Lyle Revel speaking?'

'One and the same, Nick. I was hoping we might compare notes.'

'Lyle, it's always good to catch up with you. Deveril has been like a bear with a sore head since he was assigned the task of investigating the Tube murders. Am I right in thinking you've already solved the case, you incorrigible show-off?'

'No such luck, Nick.' Lyle spoke at length about his and Hermione's involvement in the case and concluded by saying, 'Hermione and I think it's possible that Reggie Dalloway was blackmailing Vortex because he saw one of their members kill Fenella Lloyd or Oscar Sinclair.'

'You're a good man, Lyle,' Nicholas

said admiringly. 'Now we've got a possible lead, we'll check out Reggie Dalloway's bank account and see if Vortex has made a recent deposit.'

'Did the CCTV cameras at Bond Street Tube Station catch his murder on video?' Lyle asked.

'Sadly not,' Nicholas confided. 'Some drunken fool with a group of equally inebriated friends went through the station earlier last night. The aforementioned fool decided it would be a good idea to punch the camera. The camera recorded a picture of the wretched ceiling. Otherwise we would have got a brilliant shot of the killer pushing Reggie Dalloway under the train.' He broke off suddenly and a series of muffled background sounds reached Lyle. 'My God, I don't believe it.'

'What is it, Nick?'

'Word's just come in. There's been a fourth murder this morning. This time at King's Cross Tube Station.'

Lyle's heart missed a beat. 'Was the victim a man or woman?'

'A woman.'

'My God — I wonder if she was Reggie Dalloway's girlfriend?'

'That's all I know,' DS Nicholas Snare replied. 'Just how certain are you that his girlfriend was blackmailing Vortex?'

The colour drained from Lyle's face. 'Nick, I can't be certain of anything at present.'

Hermione came out of the bedroom as he hung up. She was wearing her uniform, which was even more unflattering on her slender frame than she'd predicted. 'What is it?' she asked, observing the look on Lyle's face.

'There's been another murder.'

'Oh my God . . . '

'Hermione, if you're having second doubts about going uncover . . . '

Hermione heard the anxiety in Lyle's voice and her chin rose defiantly. 'I made a promise to Peter and I intend to keep it.'

'At the slightest hint of danger, I want you to jump on the next train and get the hell out of Pembroke Grove.'

'Stop worrying.' Hermione spoke with far more reassurance than she was feeling.

'I don't intend for my first day on London Underground to be my last.'

★ ★ ★

'Vortex is incredibly dangerous. You mustn't take any unnecessary risks. They've already killed four people.'

Lyle's warning was uppermost in Hermione's mind as she alighted from the double-decker bus that had brought her from central London to Pembroke Gove. She was standing on the pavement by a bus stop beneath the railway underpass. Only forty-five percent of the London Underground railway network was situated in tunnels beneath the ground. She looked up as a train roared past overhead. The West London branch line was built on a viaduct, and passengers travelling between Tooting Wood and Paddington Central were able to view the surrounding neighbourhood from the windows of the train.

Beneath the underpass, numerous retail shops lined either side of the road, which shared the same name as the Tube station, the entrance to which was fifty yards from the bus stop. Hermione entered the cold, dank ticket hall. There was no ticket office on the station. Customers had a choice of buying their tickets online, or they could use the three self-service machines in the ticket hall. She saw a young black station assistant filling a leaflet rack with a fresh supply of Tube maps. He was in his early twenties, with a square jaw and a mane of long braided hair that was secured in a ponytail.

'Are you Hermione Bradbury?' he asked, looking up with a gap-toothed smile.

'Yes — I'm on the graduate trainee programme.'

'I'm Jacob Adefami, one of the station assistants rostered here at Pembroke Grove.'

His friendly, easy-going manner suggested he was happy with his life and at peace with his fellow human beings. But Hermione knew only too well that appearances could be deceptive. If Peter Hamilton was right, Pembroke Grove

Tube Station was the hub of Vortex's terrorist activities.

'I'm looking forward to working here,' she said. 'Everyone I've spoken to says this is a busy station. But it doesn't seem busy at the moment.'

Jacob chuckled. 'That's the way we like it, believe me. The ticket hall is very busy during the morning and evening rush hours.'

Jacob led the way upstairs to a landing where the stairs forked. The signage on the wall indicated that one flight of stairs led to the westbound platform while the other led to the station control room and staff accommodation on the eastbound platform. Hermione followed Jacob along a passageway, flanked with advertising posters, up a second flight of steps and onto the eastbound platform. Coming along the platform towards them, wearing a station supervisor's uniform, was the last person she was expecting to see — Ashley Brockman.

Hermione's shock and disbelief turned quickly to anger. Ashley and Julia Brockman were the worst caretakers

Milsham Castle had ever had, she thought indignantly. Suddenly all her suspicions about Ashley Brockman crystalized in her mind, and everything fell into place with a click. Ashley must have been working for London Underground all along. That would explain the reason for his furtive trips to London, why he was so lazy around Milsham Castle, and why Julia was always making excuses for his absences. She and Lyle were right to suspect they'd been lying. Of all the coincidences — to come face to face with Ashley Brockman again. Hermione attempted to reassure herself that coincidence plays a greater part in life than people realize, but her heart was pounding and she fought down a sense of rising panic.

'Hello, Hermione. Welcome to Pembroke Grove,' Ashley said in a calm voice. Turning to his station assistant, he added, 'Jacob, could you return to the ticket hall, please? I'll give a shout on the radio if I need anything.'

Jacob immediately obeyed him. Hermione was surprised by the edge of authority in Ashley's voice. He was of medium height, with a barrel chest, a leathery-looking face and dark unruly hair. His eyes, hard with suspicion, stared at her. The uniform he was wearing emphasized an air of aggressive determination that she had never noticed in him before now. It occurred to Hermione that he would make a formidable adversary. Was he also the driving force behind Vortex?

Ashley asked with a noticeable lack of friendliness in his voice, 'What are you doing here?'

'Lyle and I have split up,' Hermione said. 'I warned him not to go on seeing other women behind my back — '

'Only he didn't listen.' Ashley's tone implied sympathy. 'You're an attractive woman, Hermione. I'm sorry your relationship with him didn't work out. There are better men around than Lyle.'

Ashley's smile showed off an excellent set of white teeth. Hermione remembered that his smile and glib, reassuring voice were his two strongest assets.

'This is the first station I've worked on,' she said, 'since joining London Underground's graduate trainee scheme. I'm hoping to learn a lot.'

'The staff will do their utmost to make your time here with us pleasant, Hermione.'

She wondered if there was a threat behind his words. Her plan to infiltrate Vortex was almost certainly going to depend on whether she could disarm his suspicions of her.

Ashley's eyes narrowed. 'Why aren't you supporting yourself by playing the cello?'

'I've been diagnosed with repetitive strain injury. My doctor says the only way to get rid of it is to give it up for a year.' Hermione's story sounded extremely convincing because she had, in fact, once suffered from the condition and had made a full recovery. 'There's no cure for it, I'm afraid,' she added with a sigh. 'It's possible I may never play the cello again.'

'That's too bad,' Ashley said with a noticeable lack of sympathy.

'How long have you worked for London Underground?'

'Ten years,' came his reluctant reply.

'London Underground would fire you

instantly if they found out you'd also been employed by Lord Milsham,' Hermione said. 'Having a second job of any description violates your contract with the company.'

Ashley regarded her with a wary set of eyes. 'I'd be grateful if you could keep the fact to yourself.'

Conscious of the extraordinary tension between them, Hermione said, 'I need your help in passing the graduate trainee scheme.'

Ashley said swiftly, 'I'll give you as much help as you need, Hermione.'

'And in return I promise not to tell anyone you and Julia were caretakers at Milsham Castle,' she said, feigning relief at having made a deal with him. 'I'm not in the habit of throwing myself on the mercy of others, but I could really do with your help.'

Again that personable smile. It occurred to Hermione that Ashley was attracted to her. She shook hands with him and was disconcerted by the strength of his grip.

'We have a deal, Hermione.'

'How's Julia?'

'She's doing OK.' The quietness of Ashley's voice indicated he disliked being questioned about his wife. He added after a pause, 'Things are rather difficult for us at present — even more so than usual.'

'In what way?'

'Julia suffers from bad nerves. Thanks to her overspending, our finances are in a terrible state. That's why I was forced to take on a second job working for Lord Milsham. She and I are really grateful to Lyle and you for giving us the use of the South Lodge in lieu of a month's notice.'

'Have you found anywhere else to live yet?'

'We've taken a lease on a cheap flat in Bayswater, but it won't be available for us to move into until after Christmas.'

Hermione nodded understandingly, although she had no idea if Ashley was telling her the truth. 'Lord Milsham has no idea about our arrangement,' she reminded him in a reassuring voice. 'Provided you move out of the South Lodge by the beginning of January, there won't be a problem. If he were to find out, I can promise you he would be mean enough to insist on charging you rent.'

'I appreciate your help, Hermione. Julia and I will be gone long before Lord Milsham returns from Switzerland.'

Hermione added quickly, 'I'd be grateful if you didn't tell Lyle where I am. There's no way I'm prepared to welcome that self-centred, egomaniacal creep back into my life. He's too possessive and is always demanding to know where I've been and who I've been with. I want a real man in my life — one who knows how to show me a good time and treat me right.'

Her mouth was distinctly dry as she gave Ashley what she hoped was a mildly flirtatious look. The smile returned to his face — he was so sure and confident of himself that she was tempted to find a way to permanently wipe the smile off his face.

'You can rely on my discretion, Hermione.' Ashley assured her. 'Your life can only improve from now on. I'll take you to the control room, get you signed in, and then I'll familiarize you with the station.'

Hermione was convinced Ashley hadn't told her the full truth about himself, but for the time being she had no choice other than to do what was asked of her.

'Just how safe is it for a woman to go about by herself in this area?' she asked with a shiver.

Ashley gave an ominous chuckle. 'There were ten known incidents of murder or attempted murder along the West London Line last year.'

'Ten?' Hermione stared at him in shock.

Ashley said matter-of-factly, 'The police came to Pembroke Grove each time to collect the CCTV video footage from the various stations on the group. This area is notorious for gangland violence.' His next words contained an unmistakable warning. 'Provided you stick by me, Hermione, you'll be perfectly safe . . . '

5

At three o'clock that afternoon, Lyle Revel and the cast of *Dead Reckoning* took a tea break at Broadcasting House. Syd Vance, a confirmed alcoholic and control freak, was directing the radio play, and his ex-wife Elspeth Barraclough, fearful of provoking one of his rages, was being surprisingly gracious to everyone. Her six-month reign on the West End stage as the play's leading lady had undergone a transformation from crusty old battle-axe to saccharine-coated saint for her ex-husband's benefit. This had led to everyone in the cast reeling with shock and amusement behind her back.

By prior arrangement, Lye had agreed to meet Peter Hamilton downstairs in the marble lobby. Their exchange took place in a corner while two officers from the police protection team kept a watchful eye on them from a discreet distance.

'What have the police found out about

the latest victim?' Lyle asked.

'Beryl Livingstone was a black twenty-four-year-old radiologist who worked at St Dominic's Hospital near Russell Square. Apparently she was a gospel singer with her local church choir and raised a considerable amount for charity. She was on her way to work when the attack took place at King's Cross Tube Station.'

'What happened?'

'She was pushed under a westbound Piccadilly Line train during the rush hour. A station assistant was doing platform duty at the time. It was his job to announce the arrival of each train with a hand-held microphone as well as signal to the driver with a white baton when it was safe for the doors to close and for the train to depart. Customers were becoming restless waiting for the next train. The station assistant didn't see the attack on Beryl Livingstone because he was halfway along the platform. The police wasted their time examining the CCTV tapes after the murder.'

'Why do you say that?' Lyle asked.

'The video recorder was broken and the cassette that was removed from the machine was totally blank.'

'Damn and hell!' Lyle muttered. 'If I didn't know any better, Peter, I'd think the gods on Mount Olympus were conspiring to help Vortex get away with these murders. We're lost in a maze with a Minotaur roaming London Underground. He hides in shadows and is impossible to detect. Sooner or later his luck has got to change. I just hope to God no one else dies in the meantime.'

'So do I.'

'Has Vortex claimed responsibility for Beryl Livingstone's murder yet?'

Peter shook his head. 'I've been waiting for their phone call with a mixture of anger and dread.' He added with a sigh, 'Last night I took three sleeping tablets, but I hardly slept at all. Knowing I'll never see Fenella again is tearing me in two . . . By the way, I spoke to my deputy this morning.'

'Were you able to find out where Daniel Fitzpatrick was on Monday morning?' Lyle asked.

Peter's voice was tight with suspicion. 'He claims he was caught up in traffic on the way to work, which is why he was late for a meeting. We've no way of knowing if he was telling the truth, or whether he killed Oscar Sinclair at Baker Street Tube Station in mistake for me.'

'And this morning?'

'Daniel Fitzpatrick didn't arrive at 55 Broadway until shortly after ten o'clock. He says he spent the morning at home. He might just as easily have been killing Beryl Livingstone at King's Cross Tube Station. Halfway through our conversation, I complained I had a sore tooth.'

'Did Daniel Fitzpatrick fall for your ruse and tell you the name of his dentist?'

'Yes — I've got an appointment for later this afternoon.'

* * *

It was four-thirty by the time Lyle left Broadcasting House. The recording session had run into a couple of technical difficulties, and this had led to delays that had stretched his patience. Hermione's

71

safety was uppermost in his mind, and he felt guilty for agreeing to let her go undercover at Pembroke Grove.

Presently, Lyle entered the premises of a musty second-hand bookshop in Cyril Court off the Tottenham Court Road and asked to speak to the proprietor. He was taken upstairs to a small cramped flat where he introduced himself to Adrian Knowles and explained that Peter Hamilton had asked him to investigate the Tube murders.

Lyle felt a mixture of liking and sympathy for Adrian. He was an intelligent-looking man, thin and wiry in build, with sand-coloured hair, a freckled complexion and a sensitive mouth. Despite his aura of grief, it was obvious he had loved Fenella Lloyd. It occurred to Lyle that Peter Hamilton must have found it hard competing with a rival who was ten years younger than him. Adrian needed little encouragement to recount the events of the previous Friday night.

'Fenella and I were planning to have dinner, then go and see a movie,' he said in a dazed tone. 'We had agreed to meet

72

up outside Tottenham Court Road Tube Station. But she never showed up.'

'You must have been worried.'

'It wasn't like Fenella to stand me up. The next morning the police turned up on my doorstep — and told me she'd been murdered.' Adrian's face convulsed with emotion and he took several moments to capture his breath. 'I could hardly bring myself to believe it. W-was someone stalking her? Is that what the police think?'

'Why do you say that?'

'She complained of being jostled by a man at Piccadilly Circus Tube Station.'

'When was this?'

'Last Wednesday morning.'

Lyle's pulse quickened. 'That's two days before she was killed.'

'Fenella was on her way to work at the time,' Adrian continued. 'I ought to have mentioned the matter to the police, but the news of her murder sent me into an emotional tail-spin. It's — it's only just come back to me while we were talking. Her death has come as a terrible blow to me. I — I don't know if I'll ever get over it.'

'Did Fenella tell you anything else about the incident?' Lyle asked.

'The man who jostled her was wearing a well-cut suit,' Adrian recalled. 'That's what surprised her more than anything, I think.'

Lyle said gravely, 'The incident Fenella described might actually have been an attempt on her life that backfired.'

Adrian's eyes widened in shock. 'You mean the killer wasn't successful until he tried again on Friday evening?'

'It's a distinct possibility,' Lyle said, taking his wallet out of his pocket. On the previous night, as part of Hermione's unofficial induction to London Underground, Peter Hamilton had given her a copy of the company's in-house magazine, *Every Journey Matters*. The latest issue featured a financial report by his deputy Daniel Fitzpatrick and a picture of him wearing a navy pinstripe suit. Lyle had cut Daniel Fitzpatrick's picture out of the magazine and put it in his wallet.

'Have you ever seen this man before?' Lyle asked, holding out the picture.

'No, I'm sure I haven't.' Adrian's voice

was adamant. 'Do you think this was the man who was stalking Fenella?'

'The police are investigating a number of possible leads.'

'It — it seems almost impossible to believe,' Adrian said, swallowing hard. 'He looks so respectable.'

'It's imperative you tell the police about Fenella's brush with death at Piccadilly Circus. There could be vital CCTV footage of the incident that could help the police identify Vortex.'

'W-what's going on?'

'That's what I'm hoping to find out.'

★ ★ ★

On Lyle's return to Claridge's, a plan had formed in his mind. He had no way of knowing for certain whether Reggie Dalloway had been blackmailing Vortex. But in the event he had sold theatre tickets to one of Vortex's members, there was bound to be a record of the fact.

A female employee of Gala Theatre Tickets was sitting behind the desk. Lyle had seen her earlier that morning, serving customers, before he left the hotel. There was no one else about now. It occurred to him that she might be able to help him, provided he could gain her trust. She was an attractive elfin-faced woman in her early twenties with long shiny black hair worn in a centre parting. Her eyelids were reddened from crying, and Lyle suspected he knew the reason for her distress.

'You're Lyle Revel, aren't you?' she said in soft, bell-like voice. 'I shouldn't have to ask you because your face was on the poster and flyers for *Dead Reckoning*. I sold lots of tickets to your show while it was running in the West End.'

'We had sell-out audiences, thanks to your wonderful help,' Lyle said gratefully. 'I'm staying in the hotel for a few days. I hope you don't mind my speaking to you like this, but I was a friend of Reggie's. He and I once worked together on a film called *The Bawdy Adventures of Tom Finnegan*.'

'I remember him telling me.'

'Are you Joyceline Pringle?' Lyle asked, reading the name badge on the lapel of her jacket.

The other nodded. 'Most people call me Carly.' She added with a good-humoured grimace, 'Having a name like Joyceline Pringle sounds too jolly hockey-sticks by half. Reggie loved teasing me about it.'

'I expect you're as upset over his death as I am,' Lyle continued.

Carly nodded. 'Reggie's work colleagues are so shocked. We're going to miss him so much. He was such a lovely man. We met just over a year ago through a part-time photography course. My brother died earlier this year, and Reggie was so kind and understanding. He really couldn't have been nicer to me. He also had a relative who died after an oophorectomy led to post-operative complications. Reggie took me on a holiday with him to Egypt to cheer me up. I didn't think it was a good idea at the time, but we both agreed after-wards that it was the most enjoyable holiday either of us had ever had. I was so upset when my boss told me Reggie had died . . .'

Lyle was adept at putting women at their ease, especially those in distress, and in less than a minute he had established a strong rapport with her. 'Did Reggie ever mention having any enemies?'

A hint of scorn entered Carly's voice. 'Reggie didn't have a mean bone in his body. He simply wasn't the sort to make enemies. There was a new lady in his life. He met her in April following his return from Egypt.'

'I don't suppose you know this woman's name or how I might contact her?' Lyle asked in a deliberately casual voice.

Carly shook her head. 'No, I'm sorry. I got the impression from what he said that the relationship was quite serious. I pray to God the police capture Vortex before they kill anyone else. I'm too frightened to travel on the Tube anymore. It's much safer to go to work on the bus.'

'You may be able to help me.' Lyle's statement drew Carly's solemn attention. 'There's a chance the killer might have bought theatre tickets off Reggie.'

Carly stared at him, open-mouthed with shock.

'Would you mind if I had a look at your account books?' Lyle saw the look of hesitation in her eyes and added quickly,

'I'm a friend of Peter Hamilton's, who I expect you probably know is managing director of London Underground. Vortex's first victim was his ex-wife Fenella Lloyd. We'd both be extremely grateful if you would help us.'

'I've got the account books here if you'd like to see them,' Carly offered. 'I'd like to help in any way I can. Vortex mustn't go unpunished for what they did to Reggie.'

She produced them from a locked drawer. It took Lyle less than a minute to find what he was looking for. On the previous afternoon, London Underground's deputy managing director Daniel Fitzpatrick had bought two tickets to see Faust.

Lyle slowly inhaled. He wondered if Reggie had found out the hard way that blackmail was a fool's game. If Beryl Livingstone was his girlfriend, and he'd told her what he knew, that would explain why she was murdered.

On a sudden impulse, Lyle bought two opera tickets to the performance of *Faust* that Daniel Fitzpatrick was attending that night at the Royal Opera House.

6

'Alpha One to all units. We have an eastbound departure from Tooting Wood.'

Darius Perkins, a man with the air of a pouncing raven, was speaking into a radio console that transmitted his message to all the staff radios on the West London Line. He turned to a machine known as the DVA and pushed a couple of buttons. Within seconds, his pre-recorded voice issued from all the tannoy speakers on the eastbound platforms situated on stations along the group.

'Ladies and gentleman, your next eastbound train has just departed from Tooting Wood and will arrive at Blackhurst Road in two minutes, Shadwell Green in four minutes, Laburnum Lane in five minutes, Whitechurch Road in seven minutes, Pembroke Grove in nine minutes, Westfield Park in eleven minutes, Oakdale Road in twelve minutes and Paddington Central in fourteen minutes.'

An hour and a half had passed since Hermione had arrived at Pembroke Grove, and the evening rush hour had descended on London Underground. She was sitting in the control room being trained by Darius. The station control room assistant was seated before a desk surrounded on either side by CCTV screens monitoring the movements of staff and customers on the nine stations under his command. Four hundred train journeys were scheduled to run on the West London Line each day. It was his job to announce every train, as well as provide customers who came to the bay window in front of his desk on the eastbound platform with travel-related information about their journey.

Despite his intimidating appearance, Darius was a relaxed, easy-going man who supported Leeds United and was only too happy to wax lyrical on the subject of his favourite football team. Hermione remembered Peter Hamilton saying he was convinced the anonymous phone call from Vortex had been made from Pembroke Grove because he had heard a tannoy message playing in the background advising customers that their next eastbound train would be with them in two minutes. It didn't require much imagination on her behalf to deduce the person responsible for making the live tannoy message had been Darius.

Hermione glanced round the control room. It was ordinary and commonplace; the last place most people would envisage as the possible headquarters of a terrorist cell intent on sabotaging London Underground's plans to privatize the Tube. The staff facilities were equally mundane: the old-fashioned water pipes in the kitchen and toilet had an air lock that caused them to rattle loudly and incessantly.

At that moment, Hermione looked out of the bay window and saw Ashley Brockman walking along the eastbound platform. She had recovered from her initial shock at finding him at Pembroke Grove. Her instincts told her it would be a mistake to underestimate him. Outside on the platform, Ashley walked past the supervisor's office, which was boarded up and strictly out of bounds to staff until contractors had removed the lethal asbestos that had recently been found in the ceiling. He opened the door of the adjacent locker room and disappeared inside. Hermione immediately heard a loud groaning noise as the door opened. A few seconds later the door closed with a thud.

The hairs stood up on the back of her neck. There was no doubt in her mind that Vortex's threatening phone call to Peter Hamilton had been made from the locker room. It was by far the quietest room at the station. She was going to have to find a way to question Darius discreetly to find out who had been in the locker room yesterday evening when Vortex had phoned Peter Hamilton.

Moments later, Ashley left the locker room and entered the control room through the interconnecting door. Sitting down at his desk, he announced for Hermione's benefit, 'That's my hourly station check over. Now all I have to do is record the fact in my log book.'

Throughout the afternoon, staff from the stations on the group radioed Darius for real-time information. He was courteous and patient in dealing with everyone's demands. It was obvious he was well-liked and respected by his colleagues.

The station supervisor at Westfield Park asked, 'Alpha One from Whiskey Papa One, where's my next westbound train, please?'

'Your next westbound train will be with you in two minutes.'

The station assistant at Tooting Wood queried, 'Alpha One, this is Tango Whiskey Three. I've got a customer who wants to go to Madame Tussaud's. Does anyone know the nearest Tube station?'

'Baker Street.'

Moments later, Darius nodded towards one of the CCTV monitors and said, 'There's trouble in the ticket hall.'

Hermione looked at the CCTV monitor in question. The image showed a group of youths fighting one another downstairs in the ticket hall at Pembroke Grove.

'Oh no, not again,' Ashley muttered.

Darius pressed the orange button on his radio console. His voice rang out authoritatively, 'Alpha One to Papa Golf Three. This is urgent. Do you receive?'

'Papa Golf Three receiving,' the voice of Jacob replied.

'Please go to your place of safety at once.'

'I'm already there.'

'What can you do to stop them from fighting?' Hermione watched helplessly as one of the youths knocked over a large information board and two other youths snatched bundles of leaflets from the racks on the wall and hurled them at each other.

Reaching for the auto-phone on his desk, Ashley said firmly, 'I'll ring the police.'

'There's no point, geeze,' Darius said placidly. 'The troublemakers will have gone by the time the police get here.' He pressed a button that activated a live microphone connected to the station's tannoy system. 'This is a message for the British Transport police officers here at Pembroke Grove. Could you please make your way to the ticket hall area to deal with a gang of fighting youths? Once again, could you please . . . '

The effect of Darius' authoritative voice was extraordinary. By the time he had finished repeating the message, the CCTV image showed the youths had stopped fighting, jumped over the gate line and fled into the street outside the station.

It occurred to Hermione that Darius Perkins would be a good man to have on her side in an emergency. A few minutes later, he stood up and stretched his legs. The time was almost five o'clock.

'Ashley, is it OK if I go for a quick break?'

'You look as if you've already made up your mind. All right, then — don't be too long.'

'Thanks. I need to call my missus.' Grinning happily, Darius disappeared next door into the locker room.

* * *

Peter Hamilton was sitting in the back of his chauffeured limousine en route to his home in St John's Wood. He was jerked out of his reverie by his ringing work mobile. A look of apprehension filled his eyes as he took the call. He switched on the speaker-phone for the benefit of the two police protection officers sitting either side of him.

'Peter Hamilton speaking.'

A new voice, one Peter had never heard before, issued from his mobile. Unlike the previous calls he had taken from Vortex, the voice of the sixth caller had an eerie, almost inhuman quality to it that was quite unnerving.

'Vortex is running out of patience.'

Peter's mouth ran dry. 'Who are you? What do you want?'

'It's imperative London Underground cancels its plans to privatize the network.'

'I won't be dictated to by terrorists, do you hear me?'

'Beryl Livingstone is dead because of you. Unless you're careful, you're going to have a lot more than four murdered commuters on your conscience.'

Anger rose up in Peter's threat, almost choking him. 'What do you mean by that?'

'If you don't believe me, then look out for the nasty surprise we've got planned for tomorrow.'

★   ★   ★

In the control room at Pembroke Grove, the door to the adjoining locker room opened and Darius returned from making his mobile call.

'Darius, what took you so long?' Ashley asked. 'Were you able to get through to your wife?'

'Sorry to keep you waiting, geeze,' Darius said with an irreverent grin. 'I know how hard it is for you to cope without me.'

Ashley laughed good-humouredly. 'Don't you worry about me, mate. I could do your job with both my hands tied behind my back.'

'Raheemah's been really worried about our dog. He's been feeling poorly. I wanted to find out how her visit to the vet went. He's going to be all right, thank goodness.'

'That's great news.'

Ashley surprised Hermione by sounding genuinely pleased. Darius sat down and pressed two buttons on the DVA that played a tannoy message alerting customers at Pembroke Grove that their next eastbound train had left Laburnum Lane and would be with them in two minutes.

'Raheemah is an unusual name,' Hermione remarked. 'I've never heard it before.'

'Raheemah's parents come from Bangladesh, but she was born here in England.' Darius pointed with his pen at the staff message board. 'There's a photo of us both on the wall. We've been together as a couple for six years now.'

Hermione gazed at the photo with interest. It showed Darius with his arm around a young woman who was wearing a black burka. 'She's extremely pretty,' she remarked.

Darius smiled. 'I'd be a rich man if I had a penny for everyone who tells me that.'

'Does she also work for London Underground?'

'Raheemah? No, it wouldn't suit her

temperament at all. She creates and sells her own line of jewellery on market stalls. She makes a tidy profit from it, too.'

On one of the CCTV monitors, Hermione saw Jacob the station assistant leave the leaflet storeroom, which had served as his place of safety when the youths had trashed the entrance hall a short while ago, and make his way upstairs to the eastbound platform. Less than a minute later, he looked through the control room window and grinned at them as he walked past. He stopped outside the main entrance door and pressed a button on the intercom. The entry phone buzzed on the desk near Darius, and he pushed a button that released the lock on the lobby door.

Outside on the eastbound platform, Jacob heard the lock being released, pushed open the door and entered the lobby. Directly ahead of him was a door with the word 'Toilet' on it. To the left of the lobby was a door marked 'Staff Kitchen' while to the right was the door leading into the control room. He pushed this open and sauntered through.

Jacob laughed. 'Did you see what happened in the ticket hall? What were those crazy nutters playing at? Is it OK if I go on my break, Ashley?'

'You might as well,' Ashley replied. 'There's no point putting yourself at risk on the gate-line in case those yobs come back.'

Jacob clapped his hand against his trouser pocket and cursed. 'I can't believe I've come all the way up here and left my mobile in the leaflet room,' he groaned. 'I need my head examined.'

'Try getting a lobotomy instead.'

Jacob accepted Darius's teasing with good humour. 'That would defeat the purpose of me checking my text messages, wouldn't it?'

'Did you lock the door of the leaflet room?' Ashley asked.

'Yeah, my mobile should be safe until I go back down.' Jacob helped himself to a cup of water from the cooler.

Ashley unfolded a copy of the *Evening Herald* that was lying on his desk. The headline was stark and uncompromising: KING'S CROSS HORROR: VORTEX

PUSHES FOURTH VICTIM UNDER TRAIN.

'Have you seen the headlines?' Ashley asked. 'The latest member of the public to be murdered is Beryl Livingstone. It says here she was a radiologist at St Dominic's Hospital.'

'Have any witnesses come forward to offer a description of the killer?' Darius asked.

Ashley shook his head. 'I would have still been in bed when she was killed. What makes me angry is the way the newspapers are blaming us for the murders. A violent splinter group of the RMT called Vortex is claiming responsibility for the murders. It says here that Vortex is opposed to privatization.'

'Blimey, they've got attitude,' Darius said. 'I'm a member of the RMT like you guys, but I don't hold with murdering people to get what I want.'

Ashley leaned back in his chair. 'According to the *Evening Herald*, Vortex is hell-bent on stopping privatization from going through. The RMT have got hold of several leaked memos. The private companies that are set to buy up London Underground in six months' time are also planning to axe over three thousand jobs.'

Darius's eyes flashed with anger. 'I could curse the lot of them!'

Jacob looked worried. 'A lot of staff won't be able to pay their rent or mortgages if they get made redundant. It's taken ages for my girlfriend Dayo and me to save up enough money to take out a mortgage on a flat. Privatization poses a real threat to our jobs and pensions. If we're not careful, a lot of us could end up on the dole.'

'As members of the RMT, we've been fighting against privatization for over a year now.' Darius's voice was charged with emotion. 'It's been a long, bitter fight and it's not over yet. But at least our protests have been peaceful. The same can't be said for the murdering sods who call themselves Vortex. It makes me wonder where it will all end.'

'If I lose my job,' Jacob muttered, 'I'll be tempted to join Vortex.'

Hermione was taken aback at the anger and fear that the subject of privatization had aroused in the staff at Pembroke Grove. But she had yet to discover which of them was a member of the terrorist cell. She wondered if Lyle's investigation was faring better than hers.

★ ★ ★

Lyle Revel was dining with Hermione's uncle Sir Roland Anstruther at the Wolseley restaurant in Piccadilly. The actor liked the barrister and always enjoyed listening to his store of legal anecdotes. Sir Roland was possessed of a hammy manner and a rich, fruity voice that helped keep juries awake during hours of tedious testimony in court. The width of his girth was evidence of his ample appreciation of excellent food and wine, and he listened with rapt attention to Lyle's description of his and Hermione's involvement in the London Underground murder investigation.

'It sounds a most unsavoury business,' Sir Roland remarked.

'Understandably, I'm worried about Hermione's safety.'

'She's a sensible person.'

'And particularly headstrong.'

Sir Roland permitted himself a faint smile. 'Like attracts like,' he murmured. 'I've always thought you both make an extremely attractive couple.'

'Hermione sends her love. She's jealous we're dining here tonight without her.'

'It will do Hermione good to mingle with the lower classes,' Sir Roland said with a laugh. 'She's more than up to the task.'

'I'd give anything to swap places with her at Pembroke Grove,' Lyle continued. '*Dead Reckoning* has me tied up at Broadcasting House for another two days.'

'I can't say I like the sound of Vortex,' Sir Roland remarked. 'Londoners can do without a violent splinter group of the RMT carrying out acts of murder and sabotage on the Tube. A more appropriate name for them would be Vitriol.'

'Peter Hamilton phoned me earlier,' Lyle said. 'This afternoon he had an appointment with Daniel Fitzpatrick's dentist. The latter lied about having an alibi for Fenella Lloyd's murder. The dental surgery was closed all day on Friday because of a family wedding. How would you like to come to the opera with me?'

'What's the idea?' Sir Roland asked curiously.

Lyle said, 'Before Reggie Dalloway was murdered, he sold Daniel Fitzpatrick two tickets to *Faust* at the Royal Opera House tonight.'

★   ★   ★

In the incident room at police head-quarters, DS Nicholas Snare was watching the CCTV footage of Fenella Lloyd's encounter with her suspected killer at Piccadilly Circus on Wednesday morning, two days before her actual murder. The decision to review the footage had come earlier in the night after her boyfriend Adrian Knowles had contacted the police to express his concern about the episode.

'What have our boys got for us?' DI Deveril demanded, entering the room.

DS Snare rewound the video tape and replied, 'Fenella Lloyd left her home as usual on Wednesday morning to go to work at the Natural History Museum in

South Kensington. We've located some CCTV footage that shows her entering Warwick Avenue Tube Station at 9.05. Apparently she took a southbound Bakerloo Line train to Piccadilly Circus and changed to the Piccadilly Line. Additional CCTV footage shows her arriving on the westbound platform at 9.28.'

'I want something better than that,' DI Deveril snapped.

DS Snare pressed the play button on the control panel. They watched the monitor in silence as Fenella appeared halfway along the platform and stood near the edge. The rush hour was over and there were about one hundred customers waiting on the platform for the next train. She opened her handbag and began tidying its contents. A man with his back to the CCTV camera walked towards Fenella. He was of moderate build and dressed in a dark suit.

'This is the interesting bit,' DS Snare said, pushing a button that slowed down the action. The man drew level with Fenella and suddenly stumbled against her. She dropped her handbag and involuntarily stepped backwards. He looked her full in the face as she was about to fall off the platform.

Several startled commuters called out to him. He belatedly offered his hand to her, but they were standing too far apart. All he had to do was take a couple of steps forward and pull her to safety, but the seconds ticked inexorably away and he remained immobile.

An Asian man darted forward and rescued her in the nick of time. Seconds later, a train pulled into the platform. The man in the dark suit turned away and hurriedly boarded the train.

'That was a near miss if ever there was one,' DI Deveril commented. 'Have we got an ID on the murdering son of a bitch who almost knocked her off the platform?'

DS Nicholas smiled grimly. 'Indeed we do, sir. It's Peter Hamilton's deputy managing director, Daniel Fitzpatrick.'

7

At the Royal Opera House in Covent Garden, there was a buzz of excitement prior to the curtain rising on that night's performance. Lyle Revel and Sir Roland Anstruther entered the auditorium, found their seats and sat down. Almost at once the actor saw the back of Daniel Fitzpatrick's head. The deputy managing director of London Underground was seated three rows in front of them in row G of the stalls.

'That's Daniel Fitzpatrick in the navy-blue suit,' Lyle whispered, indicating their quarry with a discreet nod in his direction.

'He looks remarkably respectable,' Sir Roland observed. 'Legend has it that the Minotaur in the maze was half-human, half-beast.'

'According to Peter Hamilton, prior to joining LUL Daniel Fitzpatrick was an East London barrow boy. But you'd never know it now from his cultivated manner and posh accent. His father was a railway man for forty years.'

At that moment, the blonde sitting next to Daniel Fitzpatrick turned and spoke to him. It was impossible for Lyle and Sir Roland to overhear what the couple were saying.

'Is that his wife?'

'Peter was saying Daniel and Sarah Fitzpatrick have only been married a couple of years,' Lyle replied.

'Attractive piece of goods, isn't she?' Sir Roland murmured.

Lyle nodded in agreement. 'Daniel Fitzpatrick certainly seems smitten with her.'

'His decision to see Faust tonight could be quite revealing psychologically,' Sir Roland added. 'It's about a man who sells his soul to the devil in return for unlimited knowledge and worldly pleasures. Power is an aphrodisiac for many people. Maybe that's why he covets the top position on London Underground.'

* * *

Three and a half hours later, the final curtain came down and the lights came up in the auditorium. The performance of *Faust* had received five curtain calls and a standing ovation.

Lyle Revel and Sir Roland Anstruther had thoroughly enjoyed the performance. Although they were looking forward to going outside and stretching their legs, they were in no hurry to leave the auditorium. Directly ahead of them in row G, Daniel Fitzpatrick and his blonde companion slowly picked up their coats and made their way towards the exit.

Lyle and Sir Roland caught sight of their quarry outside in Bow Street. A chauffeur-driven BMW pulled up and the driver got out and opened the back door. The couple were about to get into the vehicle when they were accosted by two police officers. One was DI Deveril, the other was DS Nicholas Snare.

DI Deveril barred Daniel Fitzpatrick's way and flashed his warrant card.

'Mr Fitzpatrick? I'm DI Deveril. We've spoken previously on the phone regarding the threat to Peter Hamilton's safety.'

Fitzpatrick started involuntarily. 'Has anything happened?'

It seemed to Lyle, observing discreetly from the shadows, that the deputy managing director of London Underground was suppressing a strong emotion. Was it excitement?

DI Deveril asked, 'When was the last time you passed through Piccadilly Circus Tube Station?'

'I don't remember.'

DI Deveril cut him off. 'On Wednesday morning you deliberately tried to push Peter Hamilton's ex-wife in front of a train at Piccadilly Circus.'

'I don't know what you mean.'

'A member of the public pulled Fenella Lloyd to safety as the train came into the platform.'

Fitzpatrick's brow cleared. 'Oh, I remember now. I tripped and stumbled against a woman. She actually took a step back towards the edge of the platform. A customer grabbed hold of her — '

'To prevent her from falling in front of the incoming train,' DI Deveril reminded him sharply.

'The customer overreacted.' Fitzpatrick's breath formed large plumes of vapour on the cold night air. 'I asked her if she was all right. She said she was fine. I apologised for startling her and boarded the train. She was perfectly fine when I left her.'

'It didn't look like that to me, Mr Fitzpatrick.'

'I tripped on my untied shoelace,' Fitzpatrick said, glaring at him. 'Take a proper look at the CCTV footage.'

DI Deveril said, 'Where were you on Friday afternoon around six o'clock when Fenella Lloyd was pushed under a train at Leicester Square Tube Station?'

'I was at home with my wife,' Fitzpatrick replied.

'Are you sure about that?'

Fitzpatrick glanced impatiently at the blonde by his side. 'If you don't believe me, ask her.'

'Why did you tell Peter Hamilton that you were at the dentist?' DI Deveril demanded.

'This is all rather embarrassing,' Fitzpatrick said. 'I forgot I was supposed to attend a meeting at 55 Broadway. Rather than admit this, which I probably ought to have done, I told Peter I had an emergency dental appointment. The fact is I was at home with my wife.' He glanced again at the woman by his side. 'You may have noticed she hasn't contradicted me in this matter because I'm speaking the truth.'

'I've got to get up early in the morning and take the children to school,' she said impatiently. 'If this is going to take some time, you might like to get a taxi home.'

She nodded to the chauffeur and got into the back of the BMW. The chauffeur drove away with her.

'Was that necessary?' Fitzpatrick demanded, watching the car disappear into the night.

'Where were you at nine o'clock on Monday morning, sir, when Oscar Sinclair was killed at Baker Street Tube Station?'

Fitzpatrick replied, 'Stuck in traffic on the way to work.'

'Any witnesses?' DI Deveril asked.

'I saw plenty of drivers in the same predicament but I didn't ask them for their names any more than they asked me for mine.'

DI Deveril asked, 'Mr Fitzpatrick, where did you purchase your opera tickets for tonight's performance?'

There was an infinitesimal pause before Fitzpatrick replied, 'From the theatre desk at Claridge's. I was passing the hotel yesterday afternoon when I remembered I hadn't yet purchased the tickets for tonight's performance.'

'Who sold you the tickets?'

'The man behind the theatre desk.'

'Was this the first time you had met him?'

Fitzpatrick showed mild irritation at DI Deveril's question. 'Yes, as a matter of fact.'

'Would it surprise you to know his name was Reggie Dalloway and that he was pushed under a train at Bond Street Tube Station last night?'

'Very much so.' Fitzpatrick seemed once again in total command of himself. 'My thoughts and prayers go out to the poor man's family. Are these questions leading anywhere?'

DI Deveril's black gaze was unrelenting. 'Where were you last night?'

'At home.'

'Your wife will confirm this?'

'No, I was there by myself. Sarah was visiting friends. As for this morning — '

DI Deveril interrupted him. 'Now why would you think I'm interested in knowing your whereabouts this morning, sir?'

A hint of acerbity crept into Fitzpatrick's voice. 'Because at eight o'clock this morning Beryl Livingstone was pushed under a train at King's Cross Tube Station. The miscreant who attacked her got away — no thanks to the blundering incompetence of both the Metropolitan and British Transport Police who were patrolling the station, I might add. My wife left home just before seven o'clock. I finished writing a report. At ten o'clock I arrived at 55 Broadway and spent the day in several meetings. Naturally I heard about Beryl Livingstone's murder through my colleagues.'

'Would you mind coming to the police station?'

Fitzpatrick's expression froze. 'Am I under arrest?'

'You will be if you refuse to sign a witness statement confirming your movements at the time of the murders.'

Although Fitzpatrick was careful not to voice his displeasure, he couldn't prevent his breath from steaming angrily on the raw night air. 'All right then,' he said. 'I appreciate you've got a job to do.' He stared for a moment with open dislike at DI Deveril, then added, 'I'm one of the most recognizable senior managers on London Underground. You do realize, don't you, it's impossible for me to go anywhere on the network without being recognized by staff?'

'You might have worn a disguise.'

DS Snare held open the back door and Daniel Fitzpatrick got into the patrol car. As the vehicle moved off into the stream of night traffic, Lyle stepped out of the shadows and turned to his companion.

'Quite a performance,' Sir Roland remarked.

'We certainly got our money's worth,' Lyle agreed. 'He claims to have an alibi for Friday evening when Fenella Lloyd was killed at Leicester Square Tube

Station. I wonder if we're wrong to suspect him.'

'Sarah Fitzpatrick is a hard-nosed woman,' Sir Roland said thoughtfully. 'At the first sign of trouble, she got the chauffeur to take her home. It's difficult to imagine her putting her neck on the line and lying for her husband.'

* * *

At Pembroke Grove Station, Hermione stifled a yawn and consoled herself with the thought that she only had another twenty minutes to go before the end of her shift.

One of the auto-phones on the desk in front of Darius rang. The station control room assistant picked it up and began chatting to the work colleague on the other end of the line. His account of the night's events was interspersed with laughter.

'Geeze, you're not going to believe what happened,' he said excitedly. 'Around nine-thirty tonight Jacob was downstairs on the gate-line when a double-decker bus collided with the bridge outside our station.

The impact peeled the entire roof of the bus back like the lid of a sardine can . . . Luckily there was no one on the bus . . . Normally buses can pass underneath the bridge without any difficulty, but this bus had broken down and was mounted on a towing vehicle that was taking it back to the depot . . . The driver of the towing vehicle must have got one hell of a shock when he failed to pass safely under the bridge . . . '

Station supervisor Ashley Brockman remarked to Hermione, 'Darius loves disaster movies, so he's in his element tonight.'

Hermione asked anxiously, 'Is there a real chance the bridge outside the station might collapse?'

The West London Line was currently suspended in both directions between Paddington Central and Tooting Wood. All the stations on the group were closed while engineers tested the safety of the bridge before deciding whether to run trains in passenger service over it once again.

'Anything is possible,' Ashley said gravely. 'If the bridge were to collapse while a train full of passengers passed over it, the press would go into a feeding frenzy. The bridge could take months to repair.'

Hermione shivered and wondered if Vortex was behind the bridge strike. She was watching Ashley closely, but his expression gave nothing away. 'Jacob seemed pleased when you sent him home earlier,' she remarked.

Ashley shrugged his shoulders. 'There was no point him being here, since the station is closed. The rest of the staff along the line must be delighted to be indoors with their feet up having cups of hot tea on a night as cold as this. It's rough luck on our customers who were relying on the Tube to get home.'

'It's a relief to know there's a good service on all other lines apart from ours,' Hermione remarked. 'I was half-fearing Vortex might strike again tonight.'

Ashley leaned back in his chair. 'You're right to be afraid, Hermione. Vortex is a force to be reckoned with. So far they've killed four customers. They're obviously prepared to do anything to prevent the Tube from being privatized.'

Hermione heard an unmistakable note of satisfaction in his voice. She was convinced he was the leader of Vortex, but it worried her that she had no proof to back up her suspicions. Peter Hamilton had received several anonymous phone calls from Vortex, and each time a different man had spoken to him. Who, then, from amongst Ashley's work colleagues were his co-conspirators?

Darius snatched up one of the ringing auto-phones, listened and then said, 'Right you are, mate. Thanks for the heads-up.' He hung up and pressed the orange button on the radio console. 'Alpha One to all units. We have the all-clear. The safety engineers have decreed the bridge is structurally sound and safe for passenger trains. Service will shortly be resuming on the West London Line, albeit with severe delays.'

'I hope Gary Arnott doesn't have trouble getting into work,' Ashley said. 'I want him to take me off on time so I can go home.'

'Who's Gary Arnott?' Hermione asked.

'The night-turn station supervisor. He's quite a character. Anyone opposed to privatization isn't advised to advertise the fact around him.'

'Speak of the devil, that's Gary now,' Darius remarked as a middle-aged man with sagging shoulders lumbered past the bay window on the eastbound platform. The entry phone buzzed and he pushed the button that released the lock on the lobby door. They heard the door open and slam shut behind the night-turn station supervisor, then a few moments later he shuffled into the control room.

'What's been going on?' Gary Arnott asked, wheezing asthmatically. 'Why is the station closed?'

Hermione saw an overweight, unkempt-looking man with greasy shoulder-length hair and a pasty complexion. Gary Arnott struck her as a disagreeable man, and instinct warned her that she would be unwise to get on his wrong side. His face was familiar to her because earlier in the night, when she had left the station to buy some milk and teabags from Tesco, she had passed the pub on the corner. By chance she had glanced through the window and observed Gary Arnott having a pint with a man in his late fifties. Their conspiratorial manner had suggested they did not wish to be disturbed.

Ashley looked pleased to see the night-turn station supervisor. 'Gary, you've missed out on all the fun and games,' he announced cheerfully. 'Everything is returning to normal — just in time for you to take me off.'

'You don't want to speak too soon,' Gary Arnott said with a harsh cackle of laughter as he dropped a copy of the *Evening Herald* on the table. 'Have you read the headlines?'

'We already know about the latest murder,' Ashley said with an exaggerated grimace of disdain. 'The only thing that will stop Vortex from killing more people is if the government backs down on its decision to privatize the Tube.'

'The government will never give in to terrorists,' Darius objected.

'They don't have to,' Gary Arnott said bluntly. 'Provided this glut of murders continues, the private companies won't want to go ahead with their plans to buy up London Underground. They'll be too frightened to invest in a network that's targeted by terrorists. Vortex is on a winning streak.'

Gary Arnott spoke with such vindictive assurance that Hermione couldn't help wondering if he was a member of Vortex. His ugly looks certainly didn't inspire confidence in his innocence.

'You've got to hand it to Vortex,' he added with another cackle of laughter. 'The woman they pushed under a train on Friday night was Peter Hamilton's ex-wife.'

'Gary, before I forget,' Ashley said with a warning note in his voice, 'this is Hermione. She's training with us.'

Gary Arnott turned to face her. 'Why's that?'

'I'm on the graduate trainee scheme,' Hermione said, pretending not to be offended by his brusque tone.

Rather unexpectedly, Gary Arnott held out his hand and Hermione was obliged to shake hands with him. There was a sour smell emanating from him and his hand was sweaty to touch. Behind his glasses, his eyes were like pale pebbles, hard and watchful.

'There's no point my recruiting you to

the RMT in that case,' Gary Arnott said. 'As a graduate trainee you're not eligible to join.'

Hermione's intuition told her it would probably be futile to attempt to ingratiate herself with him, but she still made an effort to be agreeable. 'Ashley was telling me the RMT and Tessa trade unions have done a lot to improve safety on London Underground over the years,' she said.

'You're damned right we have.' Gary Arnott's gaze was hard and unflinching. 'I'm an RMT representative. We pride ourselves, along with Tessa, on adopting peaceful measures to protect the rights of our union members. If there's any trouble brewing, I'm the person to deal with it.'

'Hermione is worried the bridge strike is the work of Vortex.'

Ashley's quiet utterance startled Hermione, who hadn't realized her thoughts were so transparent. 'We've had plenty of bridge strikes across the network without any help from Vortex,' Gary Arnott wheezed. 'The driver of the tow truck was an idiot for not looking where he was going.'

Hermione was glad when Ashley Brockman gave her permission to go home a few minutes later. It was apparent for all his good manners that he and Gary Arnott didn't want her around. She turned the collar of her coat up as she emerged from Pembroke Grove Tube Station. It was a freezing cold night. On the pavement outside the pub on the corner, she collided with a ratchet-faced man with a shaven head of white hair.

'You wanna look where you're going,' he said in a slurred voice. 'What's the matter? Are you too frightened to travel on the Tube, eh?' He grinned lasciviously at her with nicotine-stained teeth. 'Hell is coming sooner than everyone knows!'

Hermione hastened around the corner to where a taxi was parked discreetly by the kerb. Lyle was waiting for her in the back of the taxi. Relief surged through her. The takeaway chicken tikka sandwich she'd had for dinner had been awful, and she was looking forward to having supper with him at Claridge's.

As she slid onto the seat next to him, Lyle said, 'The police have taken Daniel

Fitzpatrick in for questioning. My bet is they won't release him until London Underground has closed to the public for the night. Who were you talking to?'

'Someone who's had too much to drink,' Hermione replied. 'He's a regular prophet of doom. I don't mind admitting I've had quite a night.'

8

Elia Toscarelli hurried down the crowded escalator at Oxford Circus Tube Station. It was Wednesday morning, and he was only too mindful of the fact that his boss Sandra had made it clear that if he was late for work once more she would fire him. It had been a mistake to text his girlfriend Lanelle before leaving his flat. His romantic heart would be the undoing of him, especially if Lanelle found out he was two-timing her with Coco and Rhiannah.

If it were possible for Elia to have captured the world with his dazzling smile, he would have already done so. With his good looks and singing ability, he was determined to turn himself into a global singing superstar. His band The Lazy Cats were popular in pubs and clubs. In two days' time they had a meeting scheduled with one of the big London record labels. It wouldn't be long now before he could give up his day job as a concierge and become a legend in the making. Fame was Elia's kind of four-letter word, and he was determined to ride on its crest and live forever.

The matrix board on the southbound Bakerloo Line platform indicated the next train was another three minutes away. Elia curbed his impatience. Until he got a recording deal, he had bills to pay and he couldn't afford to lose his job. Maybe he'd get lucky and Vortex would push Sandra under a train for him.

Elia hummed a tune he'd written the previous night to himself as the minutes ticked away, then looked up seconds before the incoming train roared out of the tunnel. Someone shoved him in the back, causing him to lose his balance. Within seconds, his world came crashing down around him and exploded in red . . .

* * *

Hermione and Lyle were taking a leisurely 'Papaya Passion Punch' scented bubble bath in their suite at Claridge's. She sighed contentedly and nestled her head against his chest. 'Do you realize we still haven't posted off any Christmas cards?' she said. 'We left them on the kitchen table at Nettlebed.'

'Christmas is grossly over-commercialized,' Lyle insisted as his hand caressed her right breast.

'If we're not careful, our family and friends are going to think we haven't bothered with them. Mrs Elliott has got a spare key to Nettlebed. I'd better phone and ask her to drop them in the post for us.'

'Have you given any more thought to what you'd like me to get you for Christmas?' Lyle asked.

'I'd like lots of peace and goodwill from my fellow human beings,' Hermione replied. 'It's extraordinary how murders have a way of following you around. I can't help wondering if it's got something to do with karma. Some people lead eventful lives while others don't.'

'We've never investigated a case like this before where so many murders have occurred within such a short space of time,' Lyle said. 'Thankfully the entire Tube network is closed on Christmas Day.'

'Meaning Vortex will have to suspend its killing spree even if only for a day?'

'That's assuming, of course, they haven't been caught and arrested by then,' Lyle said.

'It seems odd to think of Vortex celebrating Christmas with their families,' Hermione said. 'Christmas time was so exciting when I was a child . . . There was the thrill of being united with family members I hadn't seen in ages, the joy of singing carols, and the delight of waking up and seeing all the presents Santa Claus had left under the tree during the night.'

'My inner voice told me at the age of five that Santa Claus was an elaborate charade orchestrated by my parents.'

'I believed in Santa Claus until I was seven years old,' Hermione said. 'But I pretended to believe in him for another two more years.'

Lyle's eyes gleamed with amusement. 'Presumably because you thought you'd get more presents out of your parents?'

'I've got to be at Broadcasting House by ten o'clock. Before that, I thought we might visit King's Cross Tube Station. I'd like to get the scene of Beryl Livingstone's murder fixed clearly in my mind. She was murdered around this time yesterday morning,' Hermione said with a shiver. 'I feel so sorry for her and the other victims. Their families and friends must be going through hell.'

Lyle's attention was suddenly riveted by the changing picture on the television. He snatched up the remote control and turned up the sound. A news broadcaster for ITV was saying, 'London Underground has confirmed Liverpool Street Tube Station was evacuated at six o'clock this morning following a hoax bomb threat. The station remained closed for two and a half hours, causing chaos for thousands of commuters, and has only just reopened. The police have yet to disclose if any terrorist group has claimed responsibility for the incident.'

'Vortex promised Peter there was going to be further chaos,' Hermione said, gazing anxiously at Lyle. 'I wonder if this is what they had in mind — or if there's worse to come.'

★   ★   ★

DS Nicholas Snare arrived at Claridge's Hotel half an hour later to find Lyle and Hermione in the restaurant. 'Lyle, you're to be congratulated on your excellent taste,' Nicholas said, glancing at the décor and exposing his jagged teeth in a wolfish grin. 'Stay here often, do you?'

'We wouldn't dream of staying anywhere else,' Lyle said cheerfully. 'Especially since Peter Hamilton is footing the bill. It might interest you to know the cost of a room ranges between three hundred and seven thousand pounds per night. Royalty and the crème de la crème of society often say here.'

Nicholas smiled appreciatively. 'A policeman's wage would never cover a stay here.' He added jokingly, 'You'll notice I'm wearing plain clothes so as not to give the hotel a bad name.'

The waiter came up to their table and took their order, then Lyle turned back to

123

his friend. 'How's DI Deveril this morning? That was quite a reception the pair of you gave Daniel Fitzpatrick after the opera last night.'

'I thought I saw you lurking in the shadows,' Nicholas said. 'Who was that with you?'

'Hermione's uncle, Sir Roland Anstruther.'

Nicholas was impressed. 'Quite a distinguished barrister, I hear.'

Hermione said, 'Uncle Roly is the sweetest person I know, but I doubt if anyone who has been savaged by him in the witness box would agree. Lyle tells me you picked a less than hospitable night to confront Daniel Fitzpatrick.'

'It was freezing,' Nicholas agreed. 'Real Jack the Ripper weather. I've never known the cold to knife through me as sharply as that before.'

'How did Daniel Fitzpatrick enjoy the warmth and hospitality of the local police station?' Lyle asked.

'We couldn't have asked for a more co-operative witness,' Nicholas said. 'He denies any wrongdoing on Wednesday morning at Piccadilly Circus. He insists he didn't know the woman he nearly knocked under a train was Peter Hamilton's ex-wife. It's impossible to see from the fuzzy CCTV footage if he tripped on his untied shoelace or not. Our lab technicians are doing their best to enhance the footage.'

'It's easy to colour an incident in hindsight,' Hermione said. 'Daniel Fitzpatrick might actually be telling the truth.'

'Then again, he might be lying his head off,' Lyle said. 'It's the sort of scenario that could leave a jury arguing for hours before they reach a verdict.'

Nicholas said, 'Lyle, you might also like to know that Reggie Dalloway's fancy lady was a certain Sinead O'Leary. She's the manageress at the block of flats where he lived at Marble Arch.'

'How did she react when she heard he was pushed under a train at Bond Street?'

'Totally distraught. She thinks it's highly unlikely he knew Beryl Livingstone or any of the other victims. We've checked his bank account, and no one has paid any large sums into his account. You were wrong to imagine he was blackmailing Vortex.'

Lyle looked depressed. 'It was just a little idea of my mine. Did any of the victims know each other?'

Nicholas shrugged. 'It seems unlikely, but that's not something I can tell you with absolute certainty. No one is supposed to know, but the Police National Computer system has crashed. Someone's hacked into it.'

Lyle's eyebrows shot up. 'Do you suspect Vortex?'

'What possible reason could Vortex have for hacking into the National Police Computer system?' Hermione asked.

Nicholas shrugged. 'Vortex has a reputation for leaving a trail of destruction and confusion in its wake. One or more of its members could have a police record that they don't want us to find out about. There are also any number of criminals out there who would like to make our job as difficult as possible.'

Lyle sighed in frustration. 'In every case of murder I've investigated, the psychology of the criminal has always proved to be of paramount importance. Every crime has a definite signature.'

'Vortex's signature tune is to phone Peter Hamilton and the press,' Hermione said, 'and boast they've taken another life.'

'I wonder why Vortex didn't strike on the weekend,' Lyle mused. 'The answer might be of considerable importance to the solution of the case.'

'I don't see how,' Hermione said.

'Nor do I — for the moment,' Lyle said thoughtfully. 'I could be wrong, of course. Even so, there's a lot to be said for thinking outside the box. Often it's the only way to solve a crime in the absence of any physical clues.'

'I wouldn't be surprised if Vortex is drawing straws to see which of its members commits the next murder,' Nicholas asserted. 'Peter Hamilton has been rung by six different men. If one of them gets caught, you can guarantee he'll have an alibi for the other murders. How did you get on at Pembroke Grove, Hermione?'

'It was an eye-opening experience — in more ways than one,' Hermione conceded. 'My parents would be speechless if they could see me working alongside real blue-collar workers.'

Nicholas and Lyle looked at each other and grinned.

'Daddy, in particular, would be shocked to the depths of his puritanical Tory heart. For the most part, I was surprised at how friendly and direct the staff are.'

Nicholas nodded understandingly. 'I'd rather deal with the staff of LUL any day than interview half a dozen City high-flyers. Did you find out who was on duty at five o'clock on Monday evening when Vortex phoned Peter Hamilton?'

'Last night I was left alone in the control room for a couple of minutes,' Hermione replied. 'I managed to steal a look at the staff cover sheets. The same three members of staff were on duty with me yesterday — Ashley Brockman, Darius Perkins and Jacob Adefami. They're all fiercely opposed to privatization. Anyone of them could have phoned Peter on Monday evening to let him know he was the intended victim at Baker Street.'

'Who do you suspect?' Nicholas asked.

'Ashley Brockman, the station super-visor, runs the station with a rod of iron. I wouldn't be surprised if he's the brains behind Vortex.'

'And Darius?'

'I haven't come up with anything on him. He's a first-rate control room assistant. There's a photo of him on the staff message board with his arm around his girlfriend, who's wearing a black Burka.'

'Maybe Darius is wearing his girlfriend's black burka and veil when he commits the murders,' Nicholas suggested. 'It would make for an excellent disguise.'

'The same idea crossed my mind,' Hermione confided.

'Have you come up with anything on Jacob?'

'No, not yet. He's a station assistant and takes his orders from Ashley Brockman.'

'By the way, Nick, there's something you should know about Ashley Brockman. Hermione and I have had dealings with him in the past.'

'What sort of dealings?' Nicholas broke off and answered his ringing mobile. His relaxed, easy-going personality underwent a swift transformation. Terminating the call, he said grimly, 'I'm wanted at police headquarters. There's been a fifth murder.'

'Where?' Hermione cried.

'This morning at Oxford Circus.' Nicholas rose hastily from the table. 'A male in his early twenties. Luck was on our side.'

'What do you mean?'

'Vortex has slipped up this time. One of its members was actually seen pushing the victim in front of the train.'

Lyle's eyes narrowed. 'Nick, are you saying this lets Daniel Fitzpatrick off the hook?'

DS Snare permitted himself a triumphant smile. 'It certainly does,' he said. 'The real killer has been arrested and taken to police headquarters.'

*   *   *

Norwood Mackintosh had the unprepossessing appearance of a tapeworm. He was shaking and perspiring heavily. A badly tailored suit hung awkwardly on his tall, gangly frame. From behind designer gold-rimmed glasses, his pale eyes stared beseechingly at DI Deveril.

'I didn't kill this man,' he cried. 'You've got to believe me.'

DI Deveril leaned across the interviewing table. 'Mr Mackintosh, do you suffer from epilepsy?'

'No, never. Only asthma. I'm — I'm weak-chested. Highly strung. My doctor says I'm not to have any nervous upsets.'

'Ever suffered any blackouts?'

Norwood Mackintosh loosened his tie. 'I — I fainted twice last summer. It was so hot. Why are you asking me all these questions?'

'Five people have been killed on London Underground in the last four days.'

'This — this is news to me.'

DI Deveril's voice deepened with aggression. 'Their names were Fenella Lloyd, Oscar Sinclair, Reggie Dalloway, Beryl Livingstone and Elia Toscarelli.'

Norwood Mackintosh shrank back in his chair. 'All this questioning is making me feel queasy. I ... feel dreadfully stressed out.'

DI Deveril straightened up. Beneath his black moustache his smile was a ferocious blend of sympathy and dislike. In the harsh light of the interviewing room, every distended pore on his face was visible. His face was covered in a sheen of oil from his overactive sebaceous glands. Behind his back, his colleagues referred to him as the oily bull of the Met.

'No doubt your job puts you under considerable pressure, Mr Mackintosh.'

Norwood Mackintosh looked pathetically grateful for the other's flicker of understanding. 'My — my job as an accountant in the city is very demanding, yes. I — I'm under constant pressure.'

'What did Elia Toscarelli do to upset you at Oxford Circus this morning? Why did you snap and push him into the path of the incoming train?'

Norwood Mackintosh was shaking so badly an onlooker might have been excused for thinking he had a neurological disorder. 'I — I didn't mean to push him off the platform. God help me, I'm going to have to live with the guilt of what I've done for the rest of my life . . . I didn't mean to do it! I couldn't stop myself! I'm — I'm not responsible for my actions. Surely you must see that?'

Next door in the observation room, DI Deveril's boss Assistant Commissioner Leona Evans was watching the interview on two flat-screen monitors displaying the CCTV feeds from the interview room. Tall and statuesque, with a heart-shaped face from which her long honey-blonde hair was drawn back into a braid, she was a great stickler for detail and commanded instant respect from her predominantly male work colleagues. Well-mannered and gracious, she knew when to crack the whip. She demanded the best from her co-workers and never gave less than one hundred percent to the job herself.

Turning to look at DS Snare, who was also watching the CCTV monitors, she asked in her crisp, pleasant voice, 'What do you think?'

The sergeant was a less experienced officer than DI Deveril, but she respected Nicholas Snare's opinions because he was refreshingly open-minded, unlike DI Deveril, whose bigotries and prejudices often got in the way of his work.

'I think Norwood Mackintosh is too frightened of his own shadow to have committed any of these murders.'

Leona Evans folded her arms in the familiar gesture she adopted when listening intently to someone else's point of view. 'Go on, explain yourself.'

Although DS Snare fancied Leona Evans, he was careful to keep the fact to himself. 'The platform was heavily congested. Some of the crowd saw a man pushed under a train. In their horror and outrage, they immediately wanted the culprit apprehended. What we could be dealing with here is lynch mob hysteria.'

'We have three witnesses who are adamant they saw Norwood Mackintosh push Elia Toscarelli in front of the train,' Leona Evans pointed out.

'That doesn't mean Norwood Mackintosh is the murderer,' DS Snare objected. 'As we know, the CCTV footage was inconclusive. The time-delay sequence of images shows the opposite end of the platform to where the murder was being committed. Norwood Mackintosh says he was reading a newspaper and didn't see who pushed him against Elia Toscarelli. He could be telling the truth when he says he only just saved himself from also falling in front of the train. The three witnesses who saw the incident are unable to say if anyone pushed Norwood Mackintosh from behind. All they can say for certain is that they saw him pushing Elia Toscarelli. And they were frightened.'

Leona Evans nodded thoughtfully. DS Snare was right; crowd hysteria could account for what had happened. If so, she felt sorry for Norwood Mackintosh. Everyone on the platform had turned against him and pinned him down until the British Transport Police had arrived and arrested him. Public horror and outrage over the murders had reached fever pitch. The newspapers were openly critical of the police for failing to catch Vortex, and the country was bitterly divided over whether privatization of London Underground should go ahead or be scrapped. Mass hysteria had led to a noticeable rise in passengers travelling to work on buses, although necessity was still forcing four million people to use the

Tube network each day. The police and security forces were under enormous pressure to apprehend Vortex.

'I can't see Norwood Mackintosh being a member of Vortex, can you?' DS Snare added. 'What possible reason has he got to oppose privatization? Three thousand station staff are going to lose their jobs when it takes effect. That's not going to make any difference to him.'

'Thanks to the government's decision to privatize London Underground, we've got five murders on our hands,' Leona Evans said. 'There was a time when we could be proud of British Rail. That was until the private companies came along and raped and pillaged the system for their own financial gain. National Rail, as we're now obliged to call it, is a former shadow of British Rail and has been poorly subsidized for years. The standards of service and poor maintenance of the trains is despicable.'

DS Snare was surprised by her outburst. 'I didn't know you had such strong views,' he said. 'Are you saying you think privatizing the Tube will prove equally disastrous?'

Leona Evans said firmly, 'Probably. My uncle was killed in the Bexford train crash, but no one connected with National Rail has ever been prosecuted or sent to prison. The crash was blamed on a catalogue of human errors. The fat-cat bosses that run the service got off scot-free.'

'I'm sorry. I had no idea.'

'Surely you approve of the Tube being privatized?'

The young sergeant shrugged and said, 'Whatever happens, we've got to be prepared to move with the times. What do you plan to do about Norwood Mackintosh?'

'We've got thirty-six hours to question him. At the end of that time, we either have to let him go or apply to the magistrates' court for a further thirty-six-hour extension. I suggest you go next door and help DI Deveril with the interrogation.'

'Yes, ma'am.' DS Snare crossed to the door.

Leona Evans added casually, 'Have you seen your friend Lyle Revel recently?'

DS Snare knew better than to lie. 'I had breakfast with him and Hermione

Bradbury at Claridge's.'

'Let me know if Lyle Revel has any ideas that might help solve this case, will you?'

'Lyle is curious to know why Vortex didn't strike on the weekend.'

'Even terrorists take the weekend off,' Leona Evans pointed out. 'DI Deveril doesn't have to know about this conversation.'

DS Snare nodded and left the room.

Leona Evans was aware Deveril resented having a female boss. He was a male chauvinist who had been raised to believe it was a sign of weakness for a man to express his emotions, especially any that could expose his vulnerabilities. She believed DS Snare would make an excellent inspector one day, but for reasons she didn't entirely understand he didn't appear to be ambitious. There remained the possibility, of course, that he was keeping quiet about his career aspirations because he was aware that life was full of potential Iagos intent on sabotaging the progress of others. She hadn't yet decided if she was going to tell DS Snare that she was attracted to him;

but if he asked for her help in climbing the career ladder, she planned to give it to him.

A few moments later she saw the sergeant enter the interview room and take over from DI Deveril. Norwood Mackintosh was not holding up well under interrogation. He was agitated and breathing heavily.

DS Snare spoke gently. 'Mr Mackintosh, what did you do on the weekend?'

Norwood Mackintosh seemed relieved that his latest inquisitor was not as aggressive as DI Deveril. 'My bout of influenza had left me feeling unwell. I stayed at home.'

'Do you ever go to work on the weekends?' DS Snare asked.

'No, never. I'm an accountant. I have a Monday to Friday job.'

'Where were you last night?'

Norwood Mackintosh was perspiring heavily. 'I read a book and went to bed early. It seems a lifetime ago now.'

DS Snare's voice hardened. 'No one has come forward to corroborate your story. Witnesses saw you push Elia

Toscarelli in front of the train.'

'Someone pushed *me* from behind. Elia Toscarelli was in the way, or I might have gone under the train myself. I — I only just saved myself. The sound of his scream . . . was . . . terrible. Terrible. It's something I'll never forget.'

'Why don't you make things easy for yourself and tell me why you did it?'

Norwood Mackintosh made a peculiar noise and clutched his throat. Moments later he collapsed on the floor, twitching and gasping.

DS Snare turned anxiously to his superior.

'He's having a seizure of some sort,' DI Deveril snapped. 'Either that, or he's taken something to ensure the easy way out. Get some medical help. Now.'

9

At 55 Broadway, Daniel Fitzpatrick was staring in shock at London Underground's board of directors. The phone call that had summoned him from his home in Holland Park to the meeting had given no portent of impending disaster.

One of the board members, Stan Ericson-Monroe, was saying, 'We'd like to commend you on helping the Metropolitan Police with its investigation into the Tube murders.'

Fitzpatrick was careful not to show his dislike of the board's hour-long inquisition. 'As acting managing director of London Underground, I consider it was my duty to cooperate,' he said sanctimoniously.

Stan Ericson-Monroe went on, 'The board has reviewed the CCTV footage from Piccadilly Circus showing your encounter with Fenella Lloyd two days before she was murdered. You'll be glad to know the board accepts your explanation of events.'

'Then you'll know I reached out to pull her to safety,' Fitzpatrick said quickly. 'For some reason, she didn't take my hand.'

'There was a gap between the two of you making it impossible for your hands to touch?'

'Yes.'

'Did you not think of taking a step towards her to close the gap?'

Fitzpatrick felt himself breaking out into a sweat. 'As I've already explained, I wanted to, but I get quite bad arthritis. My knee locked up on me temporarily. An Asian gentleman pulled her away from the edge of the platform. It should be quite clear from the CCTV footage that I bumped into her because I tripped on my untied shoelace. At the time I had no idea she was Peter Hamilton's ex-wife.'

Jawahar Singh Savarkar, another board member, nodded his turbaned head and said, 'People seeing the CCTV footage might arrive at a more malicious interpretation. They could say you deliberately tried to push Fenella Lloyd off the platform.'

'Nonsense — utter nonsense!' Fitzpatrick spluttered. 'It just goes to show how malicious some people's imaginations are! I apologized to her for not looking where I was going and boarded the train.'

'The CCTV footage shows the back of your head,' Stan Ericson-Monroe said. 'It would have been a point in your favour if your apology had been captured clearly on film.'

'It's extremely unfortunate,' Fitzpatrick agreed. Relief surged through him. He was thinking, *Thank God the camera didn't show my face, or the board would know I didn't speak to her at all — let alone apologize for almost pushing her beneath the train.*

'We want to support you in every way we can,' Jawahar Singh Savarkar reassured him. 'Can you understand that some people might misinterpret what they see on the film?'

'I lack the malicious imagination to do so myself, but I'm obliged to accept that some people could be more deluded than others!' Fitzpatrick insisted. 'As such, I'm prepared to accept your word in this matter.'

The board of directors stared at him with an air of unhurried calm. He was being made to feel he was standing on trial in the dock at the Old Bailey.

At last Stan Ericson-Monroe said, 'Daniel, the board has decided it would be in your best interests for you to take an extended career break until the police investigation is concluded.'

For a moment, Fitzpatrick thought he must have misheard. *I'm being stood down — suspended from my duties as deputy managing director of London Underground*, he thought. *The board isn't going to find it easy to get someone as experienced as me to take charge of the company.* Through a sound of rushing blood in his ears, Fitzpatrick heard himself asking foolishly, 'But who will run London Underground in my absence?'

Jawahar Singh Savarkar's answer filled him with silent rage. 'Peter Hamilton is taking charge.'

Daniel Fitzpatrick left 55 Broadway furious at having been suspended indefinitely from his position as deputy managing director of London Underground.

London Underground's board of directors suspect me of being a murderer, he thought. *It was written all over their faces. Nothing would have given me greater pleasure than to sack the lot of them. I only wish it had been in my power to do so.*

Over lunch at his home in Holland Park, he was forced to make conversation with his wife Sarah. In the two years they had been married, she had put on weight, and the way she wore her red hair added to her matronly air.

'You might have told me you were coming home for lunch,' Sarah was saying. 'Mrs Kilburn is entitled to proper notice when it comes to meals. She can't be expected to conjure them up out of nothing when the fridge is empty.'

Fitzpatrick felt a sudden uprising of

anger. Nothing he ever did was good enough for Sarah — she always wanted more. She was constantly bemoaning the fact that her sister Cecilia had married a banker and therefore had so much more of everything than her. It was Sarah's critical manner that had prompted him to look for companionship outside their marriage in the first place.

I mustn't lose my temper with Sarah, Fitzpatrick thought guiltily. *There's no way she would have been happy to tell the police I was with her on Friday evening if she knew I had a mistress. I thought the game was up when the police accosted me as I was leaving the opera house with Vanessa last night. By an incredible stroke of luck, it never occurred to them that she was anyone other than my wife.*

Sarah asked, 'Have you seen what happened to the black burka and veil I bought Jane for Christmas?'

Fitzpatrick stiffened and said coldly, 'If you must know, I threw it out. I will not have my niece dressing up as a Muslim woman. It's a form of cultural disrespect to real, law-abiding Muslims.'

Sarah looked vexed. 'It's for her school play. The whole idea is to teach the pupils respect for other cultures.'

'I don't bloody care,' Fitzpatrick said irritably as he topped up his glass of wine. 'Muslims have never celebrated Christmas, and under the circumstances it's an entirely inappropriate gift.'

'I'm sure I can manage to buy Jane a new gift that meets with your approval!' Sarah said crossly. 'Look at what you're doing. You're spilling wine everywhere.'

Fitzpatrick put down the bottle of wine. He'd been gripping the neck of it so tightly the knuckles of his hands were white. *The job of managing director was as good as mine until that American came over here and swiped it out from under me,* he was thinking to himself. *Damn Peter Hamilton — damn him to hell!*

Sarah's voice was as irritating as a buzz saw. 'Why are you in such a bad mood?'

'There's a bloody terrorist organization loose on London Underground,' Fitzpatrick snapped. 'I'm under a lot of pressure.'

Sarah frowned suspiciously. 'Is that why

the police asked me to sign a witness statement saying you were with me on Friday evening?'

'It was nothing less than the truth,' Fitzpatrick snarled, casting an agitated look at Mrs Kilburn as she came into the dining room to clear the plates. They both declined the housekeeper's offer of coffee. The silence between them lasted until Mrs Kilburn left, closing the door behind her.

'I was going to wait until tomorrow to go to my sister's for Christmas,' Sarah said plaintively. 'But after your rudeness to Mrs Kilburn just now, I've changed my mind.'

'Sod Mrs Kilburn!' A red mist had formed in front of Fitzpatrick eyes. He felt a violent urge to strangle his wife.

Sarah stared at her husband coldly. 'Cecilia never has to put up with this sort of rude behaviour from Angus, least of all in front of the servants.'

'Do what you want,' Fitzpatrick ranted. 'I'm sick to death of you always judging me by Cecilia's standards. Haven't you worked out the real reason why your sister criticizes me so much behind my back? She's got the hots for me!'

Sarah glared at him in disbelief. 'You're unhinged.'

Half an hour later, Fitzpatrick looked out of the dining room window and watched as his wife got into a taxi en route to King's Cross Station, where she planned to take a train to her sister's residence in Cambridge. He rang the bell for Mrs Kilburn to bring him another bottle of wine, then he remembered that Sarah had sent her home. In a sudden fit of rage, Daniel Fitzpatrick snatched up the empty bottle and hurtled it into the fireplace. Shards of shattered glass scattered everywhere.

I'm damned if I'm going to let Peter Hamilton get away with stealing the top job on London Underground out from under me, he vowed. *I'm going to do whatever it takes to get it back.*

★   ★   ★

Peter Hamilton was reading a report in his office at 55 Broadway when his work mobile rang. He pressed a button on the intercom on his desk. 'Marilyn, could you please ask the police to step into my office?'

'Yes, Mr Hamilton.'

The two police protection officers who had been keeping guard outside entered his office. He exchanged a grim look with them, then answered his mobile and transferred the call to speaker-phone. 'Peter Hamilton speaking.'

The voice that came across the line was deep and gravelly, unmistakably belonging to a man whom he had never heard before. The hairs on the back of his neck stood up, because it was now apparent that Vortex had at least seven members.

'This is your friendly Vortex representative. I'm hoping we'll get along much better than you have with the other members of my organization. Because if you don't, I'll make you sorry.'

Peter had been instructed by the police to keep Vortex talking so they could try to trace the call. 'Why don't you book an appointment and visit me in my office at 55 Broadway?' he suggested.

'Another member of the public died at Oxford Circus this morning. Today is Wednesday. You've got until three o'clock on Friday afternoon to publicly announce that London Underground is cancelling its plans to privatize the Tube.'

'Are you out of your mind?' Peter snapped.

The caller's voice hardened. 'You're also going to announce your resignation and confirm Daniel Fitzpatrick has been elected to take over from you as managing director of London Underground.'

Peter's face grew pale. The public was aware, owing to a leaked memo that had been quoted in the press, that Daniel Fitzpatrick was strongly opposed to privatization. 'You can't be serious.'

'Vortex has already murdered five people. If you disobey us, the ensuing chaos will be unprecedented.'

Peter almost choked on his words. 'London Underground doesn't have a policy of being dictated to by terrorists.'

'If you try and trace this call, we'll make you sorry.'

⋆　⋆　⋆

At Broadcasting House, the recording of *Dead Reckoning* had run into difficulties. The elderly and increasingly forgetful Elspeth Barraclough had arrived on time, only to discover she had left her dentures at home in a glass of water. This shattering blow to her self-esteem, unprecedented in her sixty illustrious years as an actress, had led to her being dispatched tearfully in a taxi to collect them.

Along with the rest of the cast, Lyle was secretly delighted at seeing the old battle-axe humiliate herself. The result of the unfortunate setback was that the recording of his scenes were moved forward. He finished recording his last scene as the playboy falsely accused of murder by eleven-thirty that morning — one full day ahead of schedule. Other members of the cast would have to return to the BBC to record their final scenes tomorrow. By now Lyle was glad to be able to put the play behind him, and he looked forward to going onto new acting adventures in the future.

Tendrils of raw fog wrapped themselves around him as he left Broadcasting

House. The cold bands of writhing mist chilled him to the bone and hastened his footsteps down the street in the direction of Oxford Circus Tube Station. DS Nicholas Snare had arranged to meet him for lunch at a nearby Pret a Manger. He sniggered gratuitously as Lyle recounted the events of the morning to him.

'I gather Elspeth Barraclough isn't one of your conquests, then?'

'Not likely,' Lyle replied good-humouredly. 'It's a relief to be free of my obligations to the BBC. I can now concentrate on the murder investigation.'

'If you're so worried about Hermione,' Nicholas said, 'why don't you take her out of Pembroke Grove and send her back to Nettlebed?'

'You know how independent she is, Nick. She'd never agree to that. How's Norwood Mackintosh holding up under police interrogation?'

'He's definitely keeping something back from us,' Nicholas said. 'What's more, he doesn't have an alibi for any of the murders. He's been off work sick for a week. Influenza, he says. But he didn't consult a doctor.'

'That's hardly conclusive,' Lyle objected. 'Some people don't go to the doctor when they've got a cold.'

'Norwood Mackintosh is an asthmatic, so by rights he ought to have consulted his GP,' Nicholas said. 'Earlier this morning he collapsed under police questioning and required medical treatment.'

'What does he do for a living?'

'He's an accountant in the City with a boring Monday to Friday job. He claims he spent the weekend at home. But our lads have interviewed his housekeeper. On Saturday morning she cleaned his house at Bethnal Green. For someone allegedly at death's door, he wasn't there. Judging by the unopened mail in the letter box, he hasn't been home in several days.'

* * *

On returning to Claridge's, Lyle saw Carly Pringle seated behind the hotel's theatre desk. Business was slow and she was reading a magazine. She looked relieved to see him and pulled a photograph out of her handbag.

'Lyle, I've found out the name of Reggie's girlfriend for you. I met her earlier today. She came by the desk before lunch to say hello and take away Reggie's belongings.'

'Really? What's her name?'

'Sinead O'Leary. My heart went out to her; his death has left her so upset. She thought I might like this photograph of her and Reggie. It was taken at a pub quiz night.'

Lyle looked at the photograph. Reggie Dalloway was sitting next to a girl with long brown hair. The couple looked radiantly happy. Lyle felt angry at the way fate had so cruelly nipped their happiness in the bud.

'I'd like to speak to Sinead O'Leary. Do you know her address?'

'You're in luck — Sinead gave it to me because she'd like us both to keep in touch. I promised to let her know if I hear of any developments in the case.'

'I'd like to speak to her as soon as possible.'

'You might have to wait,' Carly said. 'Sinead left here with the intention of going to Oxford to see her brother. She was saying she could really do with his shoulder to cry on. She plans to return to London tomorrow evening. You might try her then.' She added with a shiver, 'Sinead and I were both horrified to learn there'd been another murder this morning. The Victoria Line was suspended while the authorities dealt with the emergency. Hundreds of people like me will have been late getting to work because of it.'

'By the way, did Reggie work here at the theatre desk on Saturday or Sunday?' Lyle asked in a casual voice.

'The desk isn't open on Sundays because all the West End theatres are closed,' Carly replied. 'Reggie and I took turns working on alternate Saturdays. Last Saturday it was his turn to work here.'

*   *   *

Lyle's mobile rang as he let himself into the hotel suite he was sharing with Hermione. The voice of his friend Peter

156

Hamilton sounded in his ear.

'Lyle, I'd like to meet up and discuss the case.'

'You're in luck,' Lyle said. 'My role in *Dead Reckoning* is in the bag, a full day ahead of schedule.'

'Where are you?'

'I've just got back to Claridge's.'

'Good — I'll see you there in an hour,' Peter said. 'Downstairs in the lobby. Being an American, I feel a sudden urge for a traditional English afternoon tea.'

'Peter, have you heard about Fenella's encounter at Piccadilly Circus? It happened a couple of days before her murder.'

Peter drew his breath in sharply. 'I've been shown the CCTV footage. It looks as if Daniel Fitzpatrick tried to knock her in front of the incoming train. London Underground's board of directors has suspended him indefinitely from his duties until the outcome of the police investigation. I wouldn't mind betting the evil son of a bitch is the driving force behind Vortex.'

Lyle walked into the bedroom and en suite but there was no sign of Hermione. She had spoken of visiting Oscar Sinclair's salon in Hammersmith, and he assumed she must have gone ahead with her plans.

'Have you heard from Vortex?' he asked Peter when he arrived in the lobby.

'They contacted me a short while ago, claiming responsibility for Elia Toscarelli's murder.'

'What else did they say?'

'Lyle, I've been given an ultimatum. Not only am I to announce publicly that LUL is cancelling its plans to privatize the Tube, but I'm also expected to put Daniel Fitzpatrick in charge of the company before I hand in my resignation.'

'What?' Lyle was astonished. 'Are you serious?'

'I've never been more serious in my life. The deadline for the ultimatum is three p.m. on Friday.'

'But that's only two days away.'

Peter's voice hardened. 'An emergency meeting is taking place tomorrow morning at 55 Broadway. It will be attended by LUL's Network Security team, the police and various bigwigs from the security services. Whatever the outcome, we've got to come up with a strategy to minimize the threat posed by Vortex until the police identify and arrest them.'

For someone under enormous pressure, he sounded remarkably calm. Lyle's admiration for his friend rose.

'I assume you know Vortex has contacted the media and claimed responsibility for this morning's hoax bomb scare at Liverpool Street? It's been all over the news,' Peter said.

'No, I didn't know that. Vortex's malice beggars belief. It makes me wonder where it's all going to end.'

'It's possible the end is in sight. The police tell me they arrested a man this morning at Oxford Circus.'

'No doubt it will be a great relief to everyone if Norwood Mackintosh turns out to be the killer,' Lyle said, wondering if the matter was as simple as that.

★ ★ ★

'Oscar's murder was a huge shock,' Jasmine, a twenty-year-old hairdresser at Cut and Curl, was telling her attractive client as she trimmed her long red hair.

159

'His death must have come as a devastating blow to everyone who knew him,' Hermione remarked gently.

Jasmine had been given instructions not to discuss the murder of her employer with the saloon's clientele, but she had been genuinely fond of Oscar Sinclair, and found that talking about his death eased her distress and uncertainty about the future. There was a very real possibility his wife might sell the business and Jasmine would have to find another job.

'As a mark of respect to her husband, Mrs Sinclair closed the saloon as soon as she heard that he'd been killed. He was only fifty-four — the same age as my dad.'

'What a pity.'

'That was on Monday,' Jasmine continued. 'The saloon re-opened today. 'It's not going to be the same without him.'

'I hear they were a lovely couple,' Hermione said.

'There was never an unkind word between them. Devoted to each other, they were.'

'Is Cut and Curl open on the weekend?' Hermione asked.

'On Saturdays only. Oscar usually had the weekend off. The last time he came to work was on Friday. He was booked out solid all day. Sadly, he never came to work on the Monday. His clients are going to miss him ever so much.'

Hermione paid her bill and hailed a taxi outside in the street. On the journey back to Claridge's, she added Oscar Sinclair's name to the list she was compiling for Lyle with the help of DS Nicholas Snare.

Tube Victims

Those who did NOT work on the weekend are:

Fenella Lloyd (who was murdered on the preceding Friday) and Oscar Sinclair

Those who worked on the weekend are:

Reggie Dalloway (Saturday only), Beryl Livingstone (Saturday only) and Elia Toscarelli (Sunday only)

It was all very well for Lyle to insist on thinking outside the box, Hermione thought in frustration, but for all she knew, she was probably wasting her time.

Seated before a blazing fire in the lobby of Claridge's Hotel, enjoying the accoutrements of a proper English tea with Lyle and Hermione, Peter Hamilton said, 'I spoke to DI Deveril a short while ago. He tells me three witnesses saw Norwood Mackintosh push Elia Toscarelli under the train.'

'I don't see how they could be mistaken about what they saw,' Hermione said. 'Norwood Macintosh is clearly guilty of killing five innocent members of the public. It's a relief to know his killing spree is finally over.'

Inwardly, she wondered if it was as simple as that. The police still hadn't identified Vortex and arrested its members for the various acts of sabotage they had carried out over the last six months on London Underground.

'The case isn't over until we know why Norwood Mackintosh murdered these people,' Lyle insisted. 'The man is an enigma. We know practically nothing about him.'

Peter stared at him. 'Should Norwood Mackintosh's motive bother us? The man is insane. Vortex has been leading us up the garden path by claiming to be responsible for the murders he's committed.'

Lyle strummed his fingers on the arm of his chair. 'Nothing is ever settled until it's settled right. Fenella was a forty-two-year-old palaeontologist; Oscar Sinclair was a fifty-four-year-old hairdresser; Reggie Dalloway was a thirty-seven-year-old struggling actor who worked as a theatre ticket seller; Beryl Livingstone was a twenty-four-year-old radiologist at St. Dominic's hospital; and Elia Toscarelli was a twenty-two-year-old member of the concierge team at St Matthew's Court in Vauxhall. All five victims have three points in common: they were adults and they lived and worked in London.'

'Make that four points,' Peter said. 'They all spoke English. That might be significant in some way, although I doubt it.'

'I hadn't thought of that,' Lyle said slowly. 'They don't appear to have had anything else in common. They all had different names beginning with different initials.'

There was a pause while the trio marshalled their thoughts.

'Lyle, you're looking pensive,' Peter observed at last. 'Surely Norwood Mackintosh is our man. I'm fed up with being accompanied everywhere I go by a police protection team. If Vortex was going to kill me, they would have done it by now.'

'I'm curious to know what sort of method there is in Norwood Mackintosh's madness,' Lyle said.

'Method?' Peter stared at him. 'Everyone knows serial killers don't have any method. They're unquestionably insane. It's what makes them so difficult to catch.'

Lyle said, 'It may well be that where serial killers like Jack the Ripper are concerned, the reason why their crimes went unsolved is because investigators didn't know how to interpret the clues they found.'

Peter snorted with derision. 'Next you'll be telling me all we have to do is correctly interpret the madness in Norwood Mackintosh's method and we'll know why he killed all these people.'

'At present, five questions demand answers more than any other,' Lyle said placidly. 'Is Norwood Mackintosh the killer?'

'Lyle, I don't see there's any if about it!'

Unperturbed, Lyle went on, 'What was his motive for the murders? What connection, if any, does he have with Vortex? Were his victims chosen randomly? Or did he have a personal reason for wishing to remove them? Is he telling the truth when he claims someone shoved him from behind so he accidentally pushed Elia Toscarelli in front of the incoming train?'

'The man's lying,' Hermione insisted. 'Caught red-handed, that was the only excuse he could give. Why do you have to make this case more difficult than it is?'

'My inner voice is telling me we could be looking at the murder of Elia Toscarelli the wrong way round,' Lyle said on a sudden rising note of urgency. 'I can't believe it's only just occurred to me.'

'What do you mean by the wrong way round?' Hermione asked.

Lyle reached for his mobile and

push-dialled DS Nicholas Snare's mobile number. 'I wonder if the police have investigated a disturbing possibility. Namely, whether the intended victim was Elia Toscarelli.'

Hermione's eyes widened in horror. 'Oh my God, you can't be serious.'

Peter stared at him. 'You don't actually mean the wrong person died this morning at Oxford Circus?'

Lyle nodded gravely. 'Norwood Mackintosh might have been the intended victim all along.'

10

Norwood Mackintosh left the police station in a state of nervous agitation. It had been a terrible day. After recovering from his asthma attack, he had had to wait almost two hours before his solicitor had arrived at the police station. The latter had proved to DI Deveril's satisfaction that Norwood had only returned to England from a week-long holiday in Rome the previous night and therefore could not have killed the first four Tube victims. He knew he ought to feel relief and elation at proving his innocence; instead he felt trapped in a relentless nightmare. His employer would probably sack him for pretending to be sick and taking the week off work.

People were walking past Norwood in the street, their eyes averted, almost as if they knew his terrible secret. Eddies of raw mist swirled around him like cobwebs. He looked at his hands. The blood of Elia Toscarelli was on them. Norwood felt a desperate urge to weep; to purge himself of his sin. But his heart felt as if it was frozen in his chest.

Stumbling into a café, he ordered a cup of chocolate. The liquid was wonderfully hot. On the table next to him, he saw a discarded copy of that afternoon's *Evening Herald*. The front-page headlines made him shiver uncontrollably:

FIFTH TUBE MURDER
SUSPECT HELD FOR QUESTION-ING

Norwood looked at the picture of the dead man and frowned. He had told the police that he had never seen Elia Toscarelli before in his life. But that was only partly true. When Norwood had been standing behind Elia Toscarelli at Oxford Circus that morning, he had only noticed the back of his head. Now that he was looking at a picture of Elia Toscarelli's face, Norwood had the curious feeling he had seen it somewhere before.

He started imperceptibly as his mobile rang. He saw from the caller's ID that it was Radomir. 'Radomir, thank God it's you.' Norwood was unable to control the tremor in his voice. 'I've had a terrible day.'

The familiar Bulgarian voice he loved so much sounded in his ear. 'Why didn't you meet me for lunch?'

'I'm sorry, Radomir. I completely — '

Young and petulant, Radomir never hesitated to speak his mind. The fact that he detested his job, which involved working for a pest control firm in central London, meant he was especially blunt when it came to expressing his feelings to Norwood.

'It was unbelievably selfish of you to stand me up.'

'On my way to work this morning a man was murdered under a train at Oxford Circus. It's been a lousy day. I've been helping the police with their inquiries.'

'Have the police arrested the killer?'

'No, no, not yet, worse luck. The killer pushed me against his victim. I damn well nearly fell off the platform myself.'

'You pushed the man in front of you under a train?'

Norwood heard the horror and revulsion in his lover's voice and panicked.

'No, it — it wasn't . . . I didn't mean for it to happen. The killer pushed me from behind. I — I never meant for — '

'You haven't answered my question,' Radomir said. 'Has the killer been arrested?'

'Not as far as I'm aware.'

'Does that mean they think it's you?'

'Yes, but the fact we were together in Rome when the first four murders were committed means — '

Radomir cut him off. 'What kind of sick pervert are you?'

'I'm innocent,' Norwood pleaded.

'There was a reason I wanted to meet you for lunch. Our holiday in Rome made me realize I can't go on seeing you. For Christ's sake, you're thirty years older than me.' Radomir rang off.

The colour slowly drained from Norwood's face. Every word Radomir had uttered had been like the blow of a hammer, knocking him insensible.

You're thirty years older than me.

Radomir never loved me, Norwood thought. *What kind of fool does that make me?*

He was unable to remember how long he sat staring at the window in front of him. It was clouded over with condensation. Aeons passed. He felt as if he had been consigned to a living hell. He lifted the cup of chocolate to his mouth and was surprised to discover the dregs were cold.

Words spoken by his solicitor pierced the fog of his thoughts: 'Mr Mackintosh, I would strongly advise you to go away until the police apprehend Vortex. The police will have no reason to infer you are involved in this terrible business if you're not in London.' Recognizing the importance of his solicitor's advice, Norwood dragged himself to his feet and went outside into the street.

It's imperative I get the first plane out of England, he thought. *It doesn't matter where I go as long as I get away. I couldn't bear it if I was accused of another murder.*

By a stroke of luck, Norwood had his passport with him in his overcoat pocket. His attempt to hail a passing taxi met without success. Ahead of him was Covent Garden Tube Station. He was aware the westbound Piccadilly Line ran through the station all the way to Heathrow Airport.

Although Norwood made no conscious decision in the matter, he allowed himself to be guided by his footsteps. He entered the ticket hall and nudged his way inside the crowded lift. He was conscious of the people in the lift staring at him, and he wondered if they knew his terrible secret.

Within a single day he'd witnessed a murder, the police had interrogated him to within an inch of his life, and the man he loved more than anyone else in the world had walked out on him. There was nothing left to care about. His world had fallen apart around him.

* * *

At police headquarters, Assistant Commissioner Leona Evans was on her way to the incident room following a long meeting with several heads of the Metropolitan and British Transport Police. The meeting had been a highly charged one. All leave had been cancelled because of the threat posed by Vortex. Specialist firearms officers were being drafted in to patrol the stations on London Underground until the current crisis was over. The press was having a field day, and the Prime Minister was being updated hourly on the crisis by the Metropolitan Police Commissioner.

Leona Evans encountered DS Nicholas Snare in the corridor extracting a Mars bar from the vending machine. 'Has there been any progress since I last spoke to you?' she asked.

'We've discovered Norwood Mackintosh's secret,' Nicholas said. 'Having the flu isn't the real reason he took the week off work. That was just an excuse. He went to Rome and booked into a hotel with his gay Bulgarian lover. There's no way either of them could be implicated in the first four murders.'

Nicholas took his ringing mobile out of his pocket and pressed a button to receive the call. 'DS Snare speaking.' He listened intently to his caller, then said, 'Thanks for letting me know. I only hope we're not too late.' He snapped his mobile shut.

'Too late for what?' Leona Evans asked.

'That was Lyle Revel,' Nicholas replied.

'He thinks it's possible the real intended victim this morning was Norwood Mackintosh.'

'Where's DI Deveril?' Leona Evans demanded. 'I want Norwood Mackintosh taken into protective police custody immediately.'

*   *   *

DI Deveril was reading a report when Leona Evans burst into his office with DS Snare close on her heels. 'Norwood Mackintosh could be in danger,' Leona Evans said urgently. 'Where is he?'

DI Deveril looked astonished. 'Norwood Mackintosh was released an hour ago at the insistence of his solicitor,' he said. 'I had no idea you — '

Leona Evans stared at DI Deveril in dismay. 'An hour ago!'

Unable to conceal his anxiety, DS Snare blurted, 'It's too late. We've no way of knowing where he went after he left here. He surely wouldn't be foolish enough to use the Tube again.'

Their conversation was heard by DC

Murphy as he came into the office and put a manila folder on DI Deveril's desk. 'Norwood Mackintosh passed me in the street less than two minutes ago,' he said. 'He was headed in the direction of Covent Garden Tube Station.'

Leona Evans turned to DI Deveril. 'Get hold of as many officers as you can. It's imperative we find Norwood Mackintosh before Vortex does.'

★ ★ ★

Outside in the street, it was the beginning of the evening rush hour. As DS Snare ran towards Covent Garden Tube Station, he found his progress impeded by the swelling crowds. Every instinct in his body warned him that Norwood Mackintosh was in danger.

Several police officers converged on Covent Garden Tube Station at the same time. DS Snare glanced frantically round the small entrance hall. It was heavily congested owing to the area's diversity of shops and theatres, which were especially popular with tourists. He was aware London

Underground's official entry-and-exit figures for the station the previous year had been in excess of twenty-one million.

Despite his bulk, DI Deveril was surprisingly agile and had no difficulty in keeping up with his younger colleagues. 'We'll never find Norwood Mackintosh in this crowd,' he rasped.

Leona Evans called out. 'He can't have got far. Everyone fan out and keep looking.'

The only means of access to the platforms was by the four lifts and a flight of stairs. Three of the lifts were in use. In the fourth, which was crammed with commuters, DS Snare saw Norwood Mackintosh. The latter's head and shoulders were bowed as if the weight of the world were on them.

DS Snare cried out, 'There he is!' He cursed inwardly as the doors closed and the lift began its descent into the bowels of the earth.

Flashing their warrant cards at a station assistant, who opened the manual gate for them, DS Snare and his colleagues hurried towards the stairs leading down to the platforms and trains.

DS Snare sensed he was in the presence of evil. He could smell it all around him. As he raced down the stairs, taking two steps at a time, his gut instinct cried out that Vortex was at the station, stalking Norwood Mackintosh.

★   ★   ★

Norwood Mackintosh stood on the westbound Piccadilly Line platform, waiting for the next train to arrive and take him to Heathrow Airport. His lips and throat were parched. The only sustenance he'd had all day was that single cup of hot chocolate.

A woman in the crowd was saying, 'The police arrested a man this morning.'

'It's safe to travel on the Tube again,' her companion replied. 'Nutcases like that ought to be locked up.'

Horrible, dreadful women — what did they know? He'd never been good at names. Why, then, did he feel all of a sudden as if the names of the five Tube victims ought to mean something to him?

Today I killed a man by pushing him under a train. They used to hang murderers in the old days. I ought to swing for what I did. Norwood closed his eyes in an attempt to banish his thoughts. He swayed a little on his feet. *I wish I was dead*, he thought. *How am I going to live with the guilt of my actions for the rest of my life?*

A man's voice sounded in his ear, 'Once a murderer, always a murderer.'

Norwood's eyes shot open and he turned his head. Whoever had spoken was no longer there.

'You won't find me next to you — I'm over here.'

Slowly Norwood turned and saw Elia Toscarelli standing in front of him — smiling as he walked backwards over the yellow line on the platform. Elia Toscarelli stepped off the platform. He ought to have fallen onto the electrified tracks. But some apparently supernatural force held him suspended in the air above them.

The murdered man's voice rang out, loud and clear. 'Norwood Hamish Mackintosh, you have been found guilty of pushing Elia Toscarelli in front of a train at Oxford Circus this morning. Have you anything to say before sentence is passed?'

Norwood moistened his lips. *I must be delirious*, he thought. *Elia Toscarelli can't be standing in front of me. T — there's no such thing as an apparition*. He closed his eyes and prayed there would be no one there when he looked up again.

The sound of the approaching train jerked him back to reality.

He opened his eyes.

Elia Toscarelli was gone . . .

Norwood's heart was beating wildly as he walked towards the edge of the platform. Suddenly he stumbled as the killer's foot tripped him. Dressed in a flowing black burka and veil, the killer passed quickly along the platform.

Norwood Mackintosh's scream of horror sounded like a lament for all the misery that had gone before in his sad, pathetic life. As he fell off the platform, he closed his eyes in terror seconds before the train roared out of the tunnel.

Thirty seconds later, their lungs burning with the effort of having run down 193 steps — the equivalent in height to a ten-storey building — the police appeared on the scene. The train driver was blowing frantically on his whistle.

DS Snare, who reached the platform ahead of his colleagues, turned to them with blazing eyes. What he had just seen underneath the train left him feeling sick.

'It's too late,' he gasped above the stricken screams of the commuters. 'Vortex got here ahead of us. We've lost him.'

11

' . . . The Piccadilly Line has returned to severe delays following a suspension of the line between Hyde Park Corner and King's Cross because of an earlier one under at Covent Garden. Owing to an on-going police investigation, Covent Garden remains closed, and all trains are non-stopping the station.'

It was a quarter to eight. Hermione was once again sitting in the control room at Pembroke Grove with Ashley Brockman and Darius Perkins. The message that had come over the radio console had been issued by the line information specialist to all the stations on the network. It was a bitterly cold Wednesday night, and the West London Line had very few custom-ers about on its stations.

Earlier that evening, Hermione had received a text message on her mobile from Lyle telling her that Norwood Mackintosh had been murdered. There was no way of knowing when Vortex's killing spree would end, or how the terrorists might react if Peter Hamilton failed to adhere to their ultimatum by three p.m. on Friday. Did Vortex seriously expect him to cancel plans to privatize the Tube network and resign from his position so his deputy Daniel Fitzpatrick could become managing director of London Underground?

Hermione broke the tense silence by saying, 'Do you suppose Covent Garden will be closed for the rest of the night?'

'It seems more than likely to me, Hermione, since it's now a crime scene.' A glum-looking Ashley was playing a computer game. 'Are you sure you don't want to go home, Darius?'

'No, thanks. I'm not that upset, to be honest.' Darius said quickly, 'I was at the time, of course.'

'It must have been horrifying for you being on the train that had the one under at Covent Garden,' Hermione remarked.

'Aye, you're right about that, Hermione. That's why I was late getting here for the start of my shift. I normally travel into work on the westbound Piccadilly Line and change at Tooting Wood for the West London Line that brings me here. When we got to Covent Garden, the train driver announced over the tannoy system that a customer had fallen under our train. There was pure panic on the faces of the people in the same carriage as me. The station was teeming with coppers. A lot of passengers transferred to other trains. I was glad to get an eastbound Piccadilly Line train out of there.'

Ashley said, 'You can hardly blame the passengers for panicking with Vortex on the loose. I was doing some Christmas shopping before I started work. The one under at Covent Garden caused delays to a lot of people's journeys, including mine.'

'Jacob will be astonished when he hears I was on the actual train that had the one under,' Darius said. 'He chose a good time to go on his two-day first-aid refresher course. I bet he's pleased to know he's got tonight and tomorrow night off.'

Hermione frowned as the control room assistant went on tapping his pen against the side of the desk. Was it a sign of inner agitation on his part? Or was he really excited at having committed the murder at Covent Garden on Vortex's behalf? Presently she changed the subject by asking, 'Do you see many celebrities passing through Pembroke Grove?'

'There's the occasional one,' Ashley conceded. 'Like the woman who writes the horoscopes for the *Daily Post*. Sometimes Peter Hamilton passes through here. A nearby radio station has interviewed him on several occasions in regard to LUL matters.'

Hermione frowned. 'His name sounds familiar,' she said in her most casual voice. 'In what capacity does he work for London Underground?'

Ashley laughed at her apparent ignorance. 'Peter Hamilton is the managing director of London Underground.'

'He's also the worst managing director the company has ever had,' Darius said with a fierce snort. 'The British government is reputed to have offered him money and all sorts of bribes to privatize the Tube. Ashley, have you been on this

year's Continuous Development Programme?'

'I'm due to go in three weeks' time,'
Ashley replied. 'You went last month,
didn't you?'

'Yeah, I sure did. It was a huge
eye-opening experience. The teacher who
took my class was also an RMT
representative. You're not going to believe
this, but London Underground's expen-
diture for last year outstripped its income
by over five hundred million pounds.'

Ashley stared at him in shock. 'Are you
saying London Underground went into
the red by over five hundred million
pounds?'

'That's right, geeze. The shortfall was
covered by a government grant.'

'It's an incredible amount of money,'
Hermione said.

Darius nodded and said, 'This grant
won't be available to the private companies who are planning to take over
London Underground. As we all know,
the first thing the private companies are
going to do is raise Tube fares and run
skeleton train services. Our trains will be

maintained to a poor standard. Passengers will be packed into them like animals fit for the slaughterhouse. Owing to a lack of investment in our trains and the Tube network, an accident will soon be waiting to happen. All it will take is a derailment to fulfil my prophecy, and innocent people will die. And I can guarantee this — not a single one of the greedy bosses who run the private companies will be charged with negligence and manslaughter. They'll foist the blame onto someone else and use their lawyers to escape justice. History has taught us this is always the case.'

Shaking his head, Ashley muttered, 'The public wouldn't be in favour of privatization if they knew the truth.'

'Is it true that Daniel Fitzpatrick is opposed to London Underground being privatized?' Hermione asked.

'Aye, that's right, Hermione.' Darius made an effort to speak in a calmer voice. 'We'd all be a lot better off if Peter Hamilton resigned and went back to America. His deputy Daniel Fitzpatrick would do a much better job of running the company. The RMT has strong affiliations with him.'

'Why do you say that?'

'Earlier this year, the *Evening Herald* got hold of a copy of a letter Peter Hamilton wrote to the Prime Minister. Peter Hamilton stated in the letter that he was determined to ensure London Underground was privatized before he stepped down as managing director. He also admitted Daniel Fitzpatrick was opposed to privatization because he believes the private companies will be motivated first and foremost by profit rather than the health and safety of the travelling public. Peter Hamilton's letter caused a sensation when its contents were published in the *Evening Herald*.'

'I'm not surprised,' Hermione said. 'What are you going to do if you lose your job?'

'I shudder to think, Hermione, I really do. There's no way I want to go back to being a postman. My ankles were a mass of scars from all the bites I used to get from dogs that disliked me delivering mail to their owners. The pay was dreadful.'

'You must have hated working outdoors

in cold weather,' Hermione said sympathetically.

'If you speak to my girlfriend Raheemah, she'll tell you I was always getting head colds during the winter months,' Darius confirmed.

'Do you have any children?'

Darius's laugh was strained. 'To be perfectly honest, Hermione, I'm too selfish to want children. I come from a family of eight brothers and sisters. My father was a garbage collector all his life, so we never had any money for luxuries. Raheemah and I want a chance of a decent life together, without the financial strain that comes from raising a family. I could curse the day Peter Hamilton was appointed managing director of London Underground. If I wasn't loath to spend the rest of my life in prison, I'd be tempted to shove him under a train myself.'

Hermione was shocked at the look of cold anger in Darius's eyes. Ashley saw her startled expression and flashed a warning glance at him. 'We ought to pipe down, Darius,' he said. 'We don't want Hermione thinking we're a pair of hotheads when it comes to privatization. Or worse still, thinking we're actual members of Vortex.'

It struck Hermione as a distinctly clever remark for Ashley to make. He obviously expected her to assume that no one who belonged to the terrorist cell would draw attention to themselves by making such an inappropriate comment.

Darius produced a sudden charming smile and quipped, 'Don't worry, Ashley; I didn't mean anything by what I just said. If I was a member of Vortex, I would have offered Hermione free lifetime membership by now.'

The rest of the night was to all extents and purposes quiet and uneventful. Gary Arnott the night-turn station supervisor arrived shortly before ten o'clock to take over the station from Ashley. The same sour smell emanated from him as it had on the previous night. Hermione found herself disliking him as much as she had on their first meeting.

'Have you heard about the latest murder at Covent Garden?' Gary Arnott asked with grim satisfaction. 'Peter

Hamilton is taking a hell of a knocking for his stance on privatization. Vortex won't let him get away with it; nor will the RMT and Tessa unions, for that matter. Not when our livelihoods are at stake and we've got our families to consider.'

'How's your wife Jackie?' Ashley asked unexpectedly.

Gary Arnott's expression fell. 'She needs to go to America as soon as possible. The medical treatment is going to be expensive, but what option have I got other than to take her?' He lumbered into the locker room and put his bag in his locker. After closing the door and snapping the padlock shut, he came back into the control room. 'Damn, I've left my peppermint teabags.' He returned to the locker room. Moments later, the occupants of the control room heard him curse out loud.

'What's the matter?' Ashley asked as Gary Arnott reappeared in the doorway.

'The key just broke off in the padlock on my locker. Now I can't get anything out of my locker, including the book I was reading.'

Ashley grimaced sympathetically. 'You

might be lucky and find something interesting to watch on TV.'

'There's never anything decent on the box after midnight,' Gary Arnott muttered. 'Once the last trains have gone and I lock up the station, I'm going to have nothing to do until morning. They don't call this the graveyard shift for nothing.'

*　*　*

Beneath the glow of the street-lamp, Hermione's breath rose in a vapour as she emerged from Pembroke Grove Tube Station, hurried along the pavement and turned into the side street by the side of the pub. Once again she found Lyle waiting for her in the back of a taxi.

'Hermione, say hello to Nick. He and I have already knocked back a few drinks in the bar at Claridge's.'

DS Nicholas Snare grinned at Hermione as she climbed into the taxi and it drew away from the kerb.

'My goodness, you're cold,' Lyle added as she took his hand and snuggled up next to him.

191

'I don't blame you both for starting the party without me,' Hermione said. 'I could do with a brandy to warm me up.'

'Why were you looking in through the windows of the pub?' Lyle asked.

'I was looking for my friend the prophet of doom. He wasn't there. Perhaps he's met his end.'

'How was your night?' Nicholas asked.

'The staff at Pembroke Grove are horrified by the latest murder,' Hermione replied. 'Did anyone actually see Vortex push Norwood Mackintosh under the train?'

Nicholas shook his head in dissatisfaction. 'We've got hold of some CCTV footage showing the moment Norwood Mackintosh stumbled and fell in front of the train. A woman — or at least we think it was a woman — in a black burka and veil was passing behind him. But it's unclear if he stumbled of his own accord or was deliberately tripped.'

'One woman in a black burka and veil looks a lot like another,' Hermione said. 'Supposing it was a man? Darius, the station control room assistant, claims he was travelling on the train that Norwood Mackintosh was pushed under, but we've only got his word for that.'

'I'll get our lads to take another look at the CCTV footage,' Nicholas said. 'I ought to warn you — the platform was crowded. One of the cameras wasn't working at all. The picture quality from the other two cameras was badly diminished because the lenses were covered in dust and grime that had blown in from the tunnel. There's just a chance our lads might be able to spot Darius leaving the train after the one under. If he was telling the truth, we'll be able to eliminate him from our inquiries.'

'It looks as if Elia Toscarelli was killed in mistake for Norwood Mackintosh,' Lyle said thoughtfully. 'But supposing it was Vortex's intention to remove both men all along?'

'Your inner voice is probably right, since both men are dead,' Hermione said with a shiver.

'Norwood Mackintosh would still be alive if Deveril hadn't released him from custody,' Nicholas said with a sigh. 'He's going to be impossible to work with until this case is solved.'

Hermione felt sorry for their friend. Christmas was five days away, and she hoped for Nicholas's sake and everyone else's that Vortex was apprehended by then.

'Nick, what happened to the woman in the black burka and veil?' Lyle asked.

'It's odd you're asking me that,' Nicholas said slowly. 'After passing Norwood Mackintosh on the westbound Piccadilly Line platform, she took an eastbound Piccadilly Line train to King's Cross, where she disappeared into the crowd.'

★ ★ ★

The following day around midday, Hermione and Lyle joined Peter Hamilton for lunch in his private boardroom at 55 Broadway. There were dark circles beneath his eyes, and they suspected their friend had spent another sleepless night grieving for Fenella, but his manner was surprisingly brisk and positive. Although they were no further forward in their investigations, he remained confident they would get results.

'Your inner voice has never deserted you before, Lyle.'

'There's always a first time,' Lyle said anxiously. 'Do you have the list of names I asked you for?'

Peter reached into his pocket and drew out a folded sheet of paper. 'During the last twelve months, London Underground has fired four employees,' he said. 'What's the big idea?'

Lyle scanned the four names on the list. 'What can you tell me about each of them?' he asked.

'The RMT representative and supervisor John Farrow was fired for rude and abusive behaviour towards LUL managers. Austin Miles, a station assistant, took six months off work with a fake back injury. Bertha Harris, a service controller, was dismissed for making racist comments. Jack Perkins was a train driver until he failed his D and A test.'

Hermione's heart missed a beat. 'Jack Perkins shares the same surname as Darius the station control room assistant at Pembroke Grove. It could be a coincidence, or — '

'They could be related to each other,' Peter concluded.

'What's a D and A test?' Lyle asked in a puzzled voice.

'Drugs and alcohol test,' Peter explained. 'London Underground staff can be tested any time. Staff who fail their test are dismissed immediately. The health and safety of the travelling public must come first. Substance and alcohol taking can seriously impair a person's ability to do their job properly. That's why London Underground has zero tolerance.'

'John Farrow, Austin Miles, Bertha Harris, and Jack Perkins all have one thing in common,' Lyle said. 'They were fired six months ago around the same time Vortex came into existence.'

Peter Hamilton stared at him. 'And you think . . . ?'

'It's possible that one or more of them could belong to Vortex,' Lyle said quietly. 'Vortex has at least seven members, judging by the number of anonymous phone calls you've received from them.'

'All four of them might belong to Vortex,' Hermione said. 'That only leaves another three members unaccounted for.'

'Does it?'

The insinuating tone in Lyle's voice did not go unnoticed by Hermione. 'We're not stuck for choice when it comes to possible suspects, are we?' she said. 'On Monday evening, Ashley, Darius and Jacob were all on duty at Pembroke Grove when Vortex phoned Peter to let him know he was the intended victim at Baker Street.'

'I'll pass the names of the four fired employees onto the police,' Peter said briskly.

A faint buzzing sound caught his attention. He drew his mobile out of his pocket. A symbol on the display screen indicated a text message had arrived in the in-box.

'Peter, what is it?' Hermione asked, observing his look of dismay.

'I've just had another communication from Vortex,' Peter said tersely. 'For some reason they didn't phone me this time.'

He passed his mobile across the table to them so they could read the message on the illuminated display screen: 'Privatization is a big no-no. Daniel Fitzpatrick must replace you as head of London Underground. Remember — you've got until three p.m. tomorrow to carry out these instructions or Vortex will ensure all hell breaks loose.'

Lyle's eyebrows rose. 'Vortex usually gets a kick out of speaking to you directly,' he said thoughtfully. 'I wonder why they've changed their tune.'

Hermione felt a shudder pass through her. 'More to the point, what do they mean when they say all hell will break loose? I've got a feeling they're planning to do something terrible . . . '

★   ★   ★

' . . . Following yesterday evening's murder at Covent Garden, the police are warning commuters to be extra-vigilant when travelling on London Underground. At the Old Bailey, the jury in the Atkinson libel case has retired to consider its verdict . . . '

Unsettled by the latest news broadcast about the Tube murders, Ulrica Corbett-Jones changed the radio channel to Classic FM. She was glad not to be living in

London anymore. Marrying Jeremy six months ago and coming to live in Chalfont St Anthony was the best thing she had ever done. At twenty-nine, Ulrica was a petite, youthful-looking woman with untidy ginger hair and a face that was all angles. Her most attractive feature was her blue eyes, which were friendly and trusting.

The cold December day pressed against the living room windows, and Ulrica was grateful for the heat coming from the blazing logs in the fireplace. She glimpsed her two dogs, Rollo and Toby, playing in the garden. She went on knitting a jumper for her husband. It was going to be a Christmas present for Jeremy, provided she got it finished on time. A few minutes later, the dogs began barking in earnest.

They only ever react like that when there's a stranger in the garden, she thought anxiously.

As Ulrica made her way down the hall to the kitchen, her snug-fitting cardigan, jeans and socks emphasized her delicate, gazelle-like grace. She pulled on a parka and thrust her feet into a pair of wellington boots. Outside in the garden, she walked up some stone steps and across the sodden green grass.

Rollo's and Toby's barking grew louder, and she laughed out loud when she saw the reason why. The two black Labradors had chased a squirrel up a tree. It was perched on a branch, hungrily eating a nut it had found in the garden.

Ulrica spent five minutes playing with the dogs, then returned to the house. As she reentered the living room, a figure wearing black gloves stepped out from behind the door and struck her over the head with the cricket bat she'd bought Jeremy for Christmas. Taken unawares, she gave a faint whimper and pitched forward as the scene in front of her eyes turned black.

12

There was no sign of Ashley Brockman when Hermione arrived at Pembroke Grove on Thursday afternoon. A slim woman with a pretty face and soft, shining brown hair greeted her. She exuded a friendly air of efficiency and common sense.

'Hello, you're Hermione, aren't you?' She spoke in a pleasant south London accent. 'I'm Angie Ryder, one of the relief supervisors.'

'Where's Ashley?' Hermione blurted.

'He's currently on a week's holiday. I'm covering his position until he gets back.'

Hermione's thoughts were reeling. Ashley kept quiet about having a week off, she thought. She wondered if he was planning Vortex's latest move. Out loud, she said, 'I'm sorry I'm late. The weather is terrible.'

Angie grimaced sympathetically. 'You don't have to apologize; I was late myself.

The traffic on the roads is gridlocked because of this dreadful weather. I'm just glad you've got here safely.'

'Where's Darius?'

'I was just asking myself the same question,' Angie replied. 'It's not like him to be late. The place almost falls apart without him. Jacob is attending a two-day first-aid course, which mean there's no one available to cover his shift. That leaves just you and me to run the station.'

Hermione soon decided she liked Angie. The latter's chatty down-to-earth manner had a way of putting people at ease. It occurred to her that Ashley Brockman's absence might be a blessing in disguise. It gave her the perfect opportunity to question Angie discreetly on the off-chance she might know something about him that could lead to a breakthrough in exposing Vortex.

'You're the first female supervisor I've met on the group,' Hermione remarked. 'How long have you worked for London Underground?'

Angie smiled. 'Twelve years. It's going to take me another eight years to pay off my mortgage, so I'm won't be going anywhere in a hurry. There aren't as many female supervisors working on the West London Line as there are male supervisors. But I don't mind because I actually prefer working with men. I've never been a girly sort of girl. I'd rather go to the pub and have a drink with the boys than go to a hen party.'

'I know how you feel,' Hermione said. 'There are more important things in life than discussing the latest fashion in clothes and make-up.'

'That sort of talk drives me bonkers,' Angie said. 'I get a real buzz out of working here. There's a real sense of camaraderie amongst the staff.'

Hermione wondered how the other might feel if she were to learn Pembroke Grove was the headquarters of Vortex. The bay window in front of them was clouded with condensation. Outside it was teeming down with rain, and dusk had come early. Over the next hour, the platforms became crowded with commuters. The gutter was overflowing onto the eastbound platform and water was running onto the track. It was a bitterly cold and dispiriting evening — and still there was no sign of Darius.

A short while later, Hermione was listening to the maddening rattle of the water pipes and waiting for the kettle to boil when Jacob Adefami entered the kitchen dressed in civilian clothing and a waterproof coat. He seemed his usual friendly self. Surely he couldn't be a member of Vortex? 'Jacob, I thought you were on your first-aid course.'

The station assistant grinned and helped himself to an apple from the fridge. 'The class finished up early. I've got the rest of the night off, and then from tomorrow I'm off on four rest days.'

'Is that your Santa Claus costume hanging up in the locker room?' Hermione asked.

'Yeah; I hired it from a shop near here. I forgot to take it home with me. Tomorrow night I'm looking forward to going to the fancy-dress staff Christmas ball.'

'I wish I was going but I've got to work,' Hermione said. 'I'm making a cup of tea for Angie and myself. Would you like one?'

'No, thanks. I don't approve of caffeine.'

'How did you enjoy your first-aid course?'

Jacob groaned and said, 'We had the most boring instructor ever.'

'Oh, no, how awful for you.'

Jacob sank his strong white teeth into the apple and began munching on it. 'Yesterday's class didn't get away until after four o'clock.'

'What a shame. You must hate it when you don't get a cut-away. Where did you do your training?'

'At London Underground's training centre in Cranbourn Street. It's just a few minutes' walk from Covent Garden Tube Station.'

Hermione's heart missed a beat. 'Did you get caught up in the one under?'

'No, thank goodness. I was lucky to avoid it because I rode home on my motorbike. I feel sorry for Darius; he was actually on the train that was involved in the incident.'

'I wonder if it was an accident, or if

Norwood Mackintosh was murdered by Vortex.'

'It was murder, just like the others,' Jacob said in a curiously flat voice. 'All the newspapers are saying so. The British government would do well to heed Vortex's demands, or I can promise you all hell is going to break loose.'

Hermione felt the colour drain from her face as she recalled the wording of the text message Vortex had sent to Peter Hamilton. Was it just a coincidence that Jacob had used an almost identical phrase a moment ago? She released a nervous sigh. 'Everyone on London Underground must be asking themselves when the carnage is going to stop.'

Jacob smiled. 'Vortex means business, so I can't see it being soon unless London Underground abandons its plan to privatize the Tube.'

'How long have you worked for the company?'

'Seven years. I've only been a station assistant for three. Before that I was a train driver.'

Hermione's eyes widened in surprise.

'Why did you give up being a train driver?'

'My activities as an RMT representative made me unpopular with LUL management,' Jacob replied with a flash of bitterness. 'They sacked me on a trumped-up charge. The case went before a tribunal and I won. As soon as I got my job back, I gave up being an RMT representative. I also took a pay cut and became a station assistant. You can't imagine how much I hated working nights as a train driver.'

'I'm glad you won your appeal,' Hermione said, aware of a strong undercurrent of anger in his voice.

'So am I,' Jacob said fervently. 'Living in London is hellishly expensive. Now my girlfriend Dayo is pregnant, we're going to have one less wage coming in. That's going to make it even more difficult for us to pay off our mortgage. If privatization goes ahead in six months' time, it's going to sound the death knell for London Underground workers like me.' He added with a sigh, 'Hermione, I've got to go. The sound of these clanging water pipes is getting on my nerves. Two different contractors have tried without success to get rid of the air lock, but it was a waste of time.'

Jacob said goodbye and took his leave. Hermione was left wondering if the experience of being fired and having to fight to get his job back on London Underground had made him angry enough to become a member of Vortex.

★   ★   ★

In the control room, Angie Ryder was advising staff over the radio console that an eastbound train had left Tooting Wood. She gave Hermione a grateful smile of thanks as she placed a cup of tea on the desk by her side.

From the adjacent locker room, there was a groan as the door leading from the platform opened and then closed with a loud thud. Moments later, Darius entered the control room looking dishevelled and damp. Hermione was glad nothing untoward had happened to him.

'Darius, where have you been?' Angie asked in tones of obvious relief. 'It's not like you to be late.'

Darius signed the staff booking-on sheet. 'My car broke down,' he said in a curiously flat voice. 'I had to leave it parked in a side street and catch a bus to work. One took forever to come along. The congestion on the roads was unbelievable. The road works in the area only added to the chaos.'

'Hermione and I have been really busy.' Angie sounded completely forgiving of him for his tardiness. 'The auto-phones and help-point haven't stopped ringing.'

Hermione was surprised to see a smear of black grease on Darius's right hand. 'You look half-frozen,' she observed in a sympathetic voice.

'Aye, it's freezing outside.' Darius rubbed his hands together to restore their circulation. 'There was no way I was going to travel on the Tube after what happened yesterday at Covent Garden.'

'I heard about the one under at Covent Garden,' Angie said, her face softening with concern. 'Are you feeling all right?'

'I'm doing fine, compared to the poor geezer who was pushed under the train. To be perfectly honest, the person I really feel sorry for is the driver. Imagine having to live with that experience for the rest of your life.'

Hermione liked Darius and wanted to believe he was innocent of any involvement in Vortex, but another part of her couldn't be sure. She wondered if his explanation for being late to work was genuine. According to DS Nicholas Snare, no one resembling Darius had been captured on videotape leaving the crowded train following the fatality at Covent Garden Tube Station yesterday evening. Was this because Darius had been the figure in the black burka and veil who had tripped Norwood Mackintosh moments before he fell into the path of the incoming train? What connection, if any, was there between Darius and the fired train driver Jack Perkins? She resolved to find out before the end of the night.

* * *

Later that night, around eight o'clock, Hermione and her work colleagues listened in silence to the unemotional voice of the line information specialist coming across the radio console in the control room.

'Over two hundred police officers have been drafted in to patrol Tube stations in the central London area following a recent series of one unders. Staff are advised to maintain a high level of surveillance and visibility as well as report immediately any suspicious behaviour or circumstances to the police. Station supervisors are also reminded to ensure their CCTV cameras are working properly and report any defects at once to the fault report centre.'

Angie Ryder burst into speech the moment the message ended. 'Flipping heck. Did you hear that?'

'Two hundred police officers?' Darius repeated in disgust. 'We're going to need more than that.'

'The majority of them will be deployed to the big stations like King's Cross, Liverpool Street and Waterloo,' Angie said.

Darius nodded in agreement. 'I reckon there will be at least one hundred and fifty stations on the network that won't have any police presence on them whatsoever.'

'It's madness to assume Vortex will only strike in central London,' Hermione said, watching him carefully. 'This psychopath could strike anywhere, any place, any time.'

'I couldn't agree with you more, Hermione,' Darius said.

'What worries me,' Angie said, 'is that Vortex might actually attack a member of staff. A lot of staff don't travel to work in their uniform. Vortex could easily mistake one of us for a member of the public.'

It occurred to Hermione that behind her strong and assertive manner, Angie Ryder was a thoroughly frightened woman. On the whole, she thought the station supervisor was right to be worried about her safety and that of her colleagues.

It was an unusually quiet night. Shortly after half-past six, a burst water main had flooded the street outside. Pembroke Grove was closed to the public at the request of the police, and trains were currently non-stopping the Tube station. The staff of Pembroke Grove were so used to dealing with emergencies that this latest operational setback had left them unfazed.

Hermione went on her dinner break a short while later. The water pipes had fallen surprisingly quiet in the kitchen and toilet. She knew they wouldn't remain silent for long — all it would take was for someone to run some water from a tap or flush the toilet, and the wretched clanging noise would return with a vengeance. While she was heating some vegetable soup, her mobile rang.

'Hermione, this is Lyle. Are you all right?'

She heard the concern is his voice and was quick to reassure him. 'I'm fine, really. Stop worrying. Everything's okay.'

Lyle heaved a sigh of relief. 'Thank goodness for that.'

'Pembroke Gove station is closed because of a burst water main outside in the street. It's rather comforting to know we don't have to worry about any of our customers being pushed under a train. I'll make my own way back to the hotel.'

'Are you sure that's a good idea?'

'There's no point you trying to pick me up in a taxi,' Hermione said. 'The police have closed the street to the public. Before I forget, there's something you should know about Ashley.'

'Why, what's happened?' Lyle asked sharply.

'There's a relief supervisor here called Angie Ryder. She's covering Ashley's shift tonight because he's on a week's holiday. My instincts tell me he's up to no good.'

'How can you be sure?'

Hermione shivered. 'Call it a hunch; a feeling. Surely you can't have forgotten Vortex has threatened to let all hell break loose on London Underground?'

'Have you spoken to Darius yet and asked him if he's related to Jack Perkins the fired train driver?'

'No, I've been waiting for a convenient moment to speak to him alone.'

Hermione heard the sound of approaching footsteps outside in the lobby and terminated the call. She looked up with a nervous start as the door opened. Darius stood in the kitchen doorway. It was impossible to tell from the relaxed expression on his face if he had overheard her mobile call.

'Angie told me to take a break,' he said with an engaging smile. 'I thought I'd make myself a cup of tea.'

'You're in luck; there's enough water in the kettle.'

'It's been a very quiet night, all things considered.' A smile played on Darius's lips and he seemed to be enjoying a private joke. 'It's hardly surprising when you consider the station is closed.'

Hermione removed the saucepan from the stove and poured her soup into a bowl. She went and sat down at the table. 'You've got some grease on your hand,' she remarked. 'I noticed it earlier.'

'Have I?' Darius rubbed his hand with a tissue. 'I must have got it on me while I was fiddling about under the bonnet of my car trying to restart the engine.'

Hermione watched him without appearing to do so. It was imperative she find out if he was related to Jack Perkins without arousing his suspicions. She waited until Darius had made himself a cup of tea and sat down at the table before she approached the subject.

'Jacob was telling me he was once a train driver. Have you ever thought of becoming one?'

'I'm happy with the job I've got,' Darius replied. 'There's no way I'd like to become a train driver. The idea of being responsible for hundreds of passengers' lives doesn't appeal to me in the least.

Especially with Vortex on the loose.'

'I don't blame you.'

'I feel sorry for all the drivers on London Underground. They must be terrified of having a one under. My Uncle Jack was a train driver. He's got a solitary disposition, so it suited him well.'

Hermione's pulse quickened. 'Does your Uncle Jack still work for London Underground, or has he retired?'

'London Underground fired him six months ago for failing his D and A test. He was totally gutted.'

'How long had he worked for LUL?'

Darius scowled. 'He devoted forty-five years of his life to working for this company — and they sacked him just like that.' He clicked his fingers with surprising force.

'It must have come as a terrible shock to him.'

'Hermione, that doesn't even begin to describe how he felt. He started off in the ticket office at Tooting Wood working alongside his wife Maureen. That's how they first met each other. After working there for fifteen years, he decided he needed

216

a change and became a train driver. It was the right decision for him to leave the ticket office, but Maureen's decision to stay working there was sadly the wrong one for her. She died from lung cancer four or five years ago now.'

'He must miss Maureen dreadfully. Why do you say it was the wrong decision for her?'

A distracted look came into Darius's eyes. 'Maureen's death left my Uncle Jack devastated. Tooting Wood was one of the first stations to be built on the network. During a recent refurbishment programme, asbestos was found in the ticket office.'

'Oh, no, your Uncle Jack must have been horrified when he found out.'

Darius spoke with real anger in his voice. 'As everyone knows, asbestos can be lethal if you breathe enough of it into your lungs. The RMT kicked up a big fuss when they found out about it. They're right to insist the company endangered the lives of all the staff who'd worked in the ticket office over the years.'

Hermione felt a flicker of sympathy. 'Is that how your Uncle Jack thinks his wife

Maureen became ill?'

Darius nodded regretfully. 'He blames London Underground for her death. I don't mind admitting he's had a bad run of luck. A year ago he was diagnosed with terminal lung cancer as a result of all the asbestos he was exposed to in the ticket office at Tooting Wood. The whole experience has left him bitter beyond belief.'

Hermione was shocked. 'I'm not surprised he's bitter. It must have been terrible watching his wife die. Why did he fail his D and A test?'

'It was his own fault,' Darius said, clenching his jaw. 'Getting up early in the mornings was hard on him. He'd warm himself up with a shot of alcohol. The company fired him for driving a train under the influence.'

'How could he have been so stupid?'

Darius shrugged. 'I wish I knew, Hermione. I can only suppose Maureen's death preyed on his mind. He's really been depressed since he lost her. Something like that would be enough to make anyone reach for the bottle. He's convinced he was fired because of the asbestos lawsuit he's waging against London Underground. Maureen's brother Gary is helping him with the lawsuit.'

Hermione's heart missed a beat. 'Are you referring Gary Arnott, the night-turn supervisor here at Pembroke Grove? Is he Maureen's brother?'

'Aye, that's right. Being twins, they were like peas in a pod in every sense of the word. Gary was really close to Maureen. He's an RMT representative. If anyone can help my uncle get compensation and justice for Maureen, it will be Gary.'

Hermione took several moments to assimilate what she'd learned. 'Your Uncle Jack must be devastated by what's happened to him.'

Darius tapped his teaspoon against the side of his cup. 'Angry and vengeful best describes his reaction, Hermione. He vowed to torch London Underground. I can't say I blame him. I'd probably feel like that myself. He lives in a council flat on a rough estate near Laburnum Lane. I wouldn't put it past him to have encouraged some of the young hooligans who live there to graffiti the walls of the

Tube station and also paint acid graffiti on some of our trains.' He saw the shocked look in her eyes and added quickly, 'Mind you, I could be wrong. I don't know my Uncle Jack that well. He's from my mum's side of the family.'

It seemed to Hermione that for someone who apparently didn't know his uncle very well, Darius was unusually well-versed on his history. 'Does your Uncle Jack have many friends?' she asked.

'There's really only his ex-brother-in-law Gary. The two of them are good mates. They're both fond of drinking. I feel sorry for my uncle. He's probably only got one or two months left to live. To be perfectly honest, I don't reckon he'll live long enough to fight his court case against London Underground.'

Hermione's memory stirred. 'Is your Uncle Jack a ratchet-faced man with cropped white hair by any chance?'

Darius eased the tension between them with a gentle laugh. 'You've certainly got a way with words, Hermione. That describes him well. Why do you ask?'

'I think I saw him having a drink with

Gary in the pub.'

'When was this?'

'On Tuesday night, when I left the station to buy some milk and teabags for everyone's tea.'

A scowl darkened Darius's brow. 'Gary should know better than to drink alcohol before coming to work. He wants to be careful he doesn't get caught or he'll end up getting fired.'

There was a moment of extraordinary tension.

'This can be our secret,' Hermione said in her most soothing voice. 'No good comes out of bad-mouthing others.'

A hint of a smile hung on the corners of Darius's mouth. 'Aye, you've got the right idea, Hermione. My philosophy in life is simple: see no evil, hear no evil, and speak no evil. Unpleasant complications are best avoided, for everyone's sake.'

* * *

At his home in Holland Park, Daniel Fitzpatrick stood in front of the oval mirror in his bedroom and admired his reflection. The Santa Claus costume was an excellent fit. He pulled the hood down over his fluffy white wig and adjusted the beard.

No one who knows me would recognize me if I walked past them in the street, he thought with satisfaction.

Silence emanated from the centre of the house as the deputy managing director of London Underground came downstairs. His wife Sarah was in Cambridge with her sister Cecilia and brother-in-law Angus. She had made no attempt to phone him after their blazing row, and he was enjoying the solitude. He was alone — his actions unobserved by anyone, free to do exactly as he pleased.

It was exactly 10:32 p.m. when Daniel Fitzpatrick entered Holland Park Tube Station.

★   ★   ★

Earlier that night, Lyle dined in his suite at Claridge's. The media's coverage of Vortex's reign of terror was close to saturation point, and he used his television remote control to flick from channel to channel.

A BBC reporter was saying, 'The Prime Minister and MPs have applauded the decision of the Metropolitan Police Commissioner Sir Thomas Pursall to draft in over two hundred police officers to patrol stations on London Underground. One and all have expressed outrage at Vortex's continued acts of violence and reiterated their determination to see the terrorists caught. So, too, have the family and friends of the murder victims. A number of special church services are being held to remember their loved ones. We now cross live to St Mary's Church . . . '

ITV's news bulletin was in full swing. 'The media has been openly critical of the police for falsely arresting Norwood Mackintosh. Shortly after being released from police custody on Wednesday evening, the fifty-two-year-old accountant was pushed under a train at Covent Garden Tube Station. Many commentators now believe he was Vortex's intended victim at Oxford Circus. It appears one of Vortex's members wore a black burka and veil to carry out the attack on Norwood Mackintosh. Meanwhile, a spokesperson from London's Muslim community, Hazeem Anwar, has expressed dismay at the police's handling of Norwood Mackintosh's murder. He said that law-abiding Muslims up and down Great Britain have joined in the nation's condemnation of Vortex's terrorist activities . . . '

Channel Five's news reporter was saying, 'Despite the public's mood of defiance and unity, fear and paranoia are rampant because no one knows for certain when or where Vortex will strike again. The idea of closing the entire Tube network until the crisis has passed was heavily ridiculed earlier today by the Mayor of London, who said the financial impact on the economy would be devastating. Not only would this mean giving in to Vortex, but it would also mean millions of people would have no way of getting to work . . . '

* * *

Shortly after eight-thirty, Lyle paid a visit to Reggie Dalloway's girlfriend. Sinead

O'Leary was the manageress of a row of run-down houses in Bryanston Street, near Marble Arch Tube Station, that had been knocked together and refurbished to form a series of one- and two-bedroom flats.

Lyle had no difficulty in gaining Sinead's trust, because Reggie had told her about the time he had worked with Lyle on *The Bawdy Adventures of Tom Finnegan*. Her shoulder-length brown hair hung round her freckled face, and she was inclined to cry a lot as she unburdened herself to him.

'Reggie and I were planning to get married,' she said in a trembling voice. 'But now I feel as if I've lost my best friend, and a hole has been ripped out of my heart.'

'Can you think of anyone who had it in for him?' Lyle asked.

Sinead shook her head. 'Reggie wasn't the sort of person who made enemies. The police asked me if I thought he might have witnessed one of the murders. But the idea of him blackmailing Vortex is ridiculous. He was looking forward to auditioning for a forthcoming West End production of *Twelfth Night*. He'd worked with the director once before and he was really hopeful of getting the part. It was all he could think and talk about.'

'How long had you known each other?'

'We met in April this year through an online dating agency called Searching for Love. Reggie and I fell for each other hook, line and sinker on our very first date. I've got a brother who's studying mathematics at Oxford. He's helping me set up a website so people can pay their respects to the murdered Tube victims. I think it would be a good idea for the families and friends of the victims to get together — to form a sort of survivors' support group.' She wiped her tears away with a tissue. 'I can't bear the idea of sitting around and doing nothing. I miss Reggie so much . . . '

'It sounds like a good idea,' Lyle said. 'It might also prove useful.'

'Useful?' Sinead frowned. 'In what way?'

'Speaking to the victim's loved ones and friends might bring to light a clue — some forgotten fact or memory that could lead to the arrest and conviction of Vortex.'

Sinead's frown deepened. 'What reason could anyone have for keeping something back from the police?'

'We don't always tell the police everything we know,' Lyle said. 'Memories can lay buried deep in the subconscious without our knowing it. Someone might have seen or heard something without appreciating its full significance.'

He felt desperately sorry for Sinead. Her grief for Reggie was still raw, and he spent almost two hours listening to her pour out her anguish. It was nearly a quarter to eleven by the time he left her. Hermione would be finishing work soon. He decided to return to Claridge's and wait for her there. It was raining heavily and three taxis passed him in the street. He winced at his bad luck. There were no sign of any buses as he rounded the corner of Great Cumberland Place into Oxford Street.

The brightly lit entrance of Marble Arch Tube Station beckoned Lyle with a deceptive promise of warmth and good cheer. He calculated that it would take him at least ten minutes to walk from Marble Arch to Claridge's in the soaking rain. Did he really want to risk catching a chill?

Lyle adjusted the collar of his brown cashmere coat and plunged down the steps into Marble Arch Tube Station. As he rode the escalator to the lower concourse, the distant rumbling sound of an approaching train reminded him of the roar of a Minotaur rising up from hell.

★　★　★

Liz Gillard was sitting in a train on the Central Line reading the *Daily Post*'s account of the latest Tube murder. Just thinking about Norwood Mackintosh's ghastly fate and that of the other victims made her shudder. She was a middle-aged woman with a meek expression and worried blue eyes. Stress had turned her once lovely chestnut-brown hair prematurely grey.

Sometimes Liz wondered what the world was coming to. Normal people found it difficult enough making ends meet and raising their families. That was without having to worry about a violent terrorist group called Vortex that was killing innocent members of the public.

She looked at the wedding ring on her finger. Without warning, a wave of self-pity almost brought her to the brink of tears. It wasn't easy having a husband who was away for two weeks every month working on an oil rig in the North Sea. She missed Desmond dreadfully, and it saddened her to know that he wouldn't be coming home for Christmas because of his work commitments.

It was half past ten and Liz was on her way to work. She was a telephonist-cum-receptionist at the Lyndhurst Club for ladies at Marble Arch. Her night shift began at eleven o'clock and didn't finish until seven o'clock in the morning. She hated the unsociable hours, the inevitable loneliness and constant sleep deprivation. She was so tired of being tired all the time. But she had the mouths of three hungry children to feed and she couldn't afford to give up her job. The money

Desmond made from working on the oil rig only just covered the mortgage on their house and the children's school fees. Ethan, Grace and Jemima were now in bed asleep and being looked after by her sister.

Sighing, Liz cast aside the *Daily Post* and looked round the carriage. Sitting a few feet away from her was a black youth. The only other passenger in the carriage was a party-goer wearing a Santa Claus outfit who had boarded the train without her noticing.

A minute or two later, the train pulled into Marble Arch Tube Station. Liz was the only passenger to disembark. She stood on the yellow line, staring at the copy of the *Daily Post* in her hand. The front page featured pictures of the six murdered Tube victims. Suddenly it dawned on her — she knew who they were . . .

Liz thrust the newspaper into her coat pocket as the doors of the train closed. Suddenly she felt a violent tug from behind. To her shock and horror, the fold of her coat had become trapped in the closed doors. She was being dragged along the platform by the departing train. She glanced up and down the platform, looking for help. But there was no one else there.

Fear lanced through her. Through the glass windows of the doors, she saw Santa Claus inside the train holding on to the fold of her coat. In a flash she realized what had happened. Santa Claus had reached out of the train and grabbed the back of her coat so the doors would shut on it . . .

Liz was aware the front of the train had already entered the narrow tunnel ahead of her. If she didn't manage to free herself before the train left the platform, she would be dragged to her death inside the tunnel. In desperation, she began unbuttoning her coat. Panic rose up in her throat like bile, almost choking her. She gave a sharp tug at the end of her belt. Her attempt to unfasten it only caused it to knot more tightly around her waist.

She banged frantically on the glass windows and gazed beseechingly into the eyes of her killer. 'Stop it — stop it . . . '

she begged. 'Please let go of my coat. Pull the emergency alarm!'

By this time, Lyle Revel had arrived on the eastbound Central Line platform. He was shocked out of his preoccupied thoughts to see an unknown female being dragged along the platform by the departing train. He ran along the platform after the woman, desperately trying to help her. She gazed at him with terrified eyes.

'Quickly — take my hand. You're in terrible danger.'

'I'm going to die . . . '

'No, I won't let you. Reach out — grab my hand.'

'I can't — it's too far!'

'You've got to try harder. Grab my hand, now!'

'I know why these people are being pushed in front of the trains,' she cried. 'It's come to me just now.'

'What do you know about Vortex?'

'The man who's doing this is out to get us all — I always said he and the other man were wrong 'uns . . . '

The newspaper fell out of Liz Gillard's coat pocket onto the platform.

Lyle ran faster, his lungs heaving with the strain of his exertions. 'Tell me their names!'

Seconds later, he saw her being swept to her death inside the tunnel.

13

At Marble Arch Tube Station, Lyle was sitting slumped on a chair in the station supervisor's office. He was drinking a cup of coffee that had been made for him by a member of staff when DS Nicholas Snare walked in through the door.

'Lyle, you certainly get around,' he said, observing the strained look on his friend's face and feeling sorry for him.

'I'm not in the mood for jokes, Nick,' he replied in a ragged voice. 'Vortex has struck again. I was powerless to do anything about it.'

The horror of seeing Liz Gillard killed was still fresh in Lyle's mind. He felt guilty for not saving her life and angry at his inner voice for failing to help him expose Vortex.

'I'd better give you the only good news there is,' Nicholas said. 'DI Deveril is not on duty. We haven't been able to get hold of him because his mobile is switched off.

That means you're not going to have to face him tonight.'

'That *is* good news,' Lyle said gratefully.

'Liz Gillard was on her way to work when she was killed,' Nicholas continued. 'You're the only person who saw Vortex's assassin.'

'There was a black man sitting inside the train,' Lyle pointed out. 'He must have seen something!'

Nicholas' reply filled Lyle with despair. 'Blind, I'm afraid. His guide dog saw more than he did. I really need more of a description from you if I'm going to catch Vortex.'

'I've no idea who our Santa Claus killer is,' Lyle said. 'His face was concealed by a white beard and the hood of his costume . . . '

★   ★   ★

In the control room at Pembroke Grove, Angie Ryder's face was white with shock as she hung up the auto-phone and turned to Hermione. 'I've just been speaking to the line information specialist at White City,' she said in a trembling voice. 'Earlier tonight a woman was killed on the Central Line.'

Hermione was stunned. 'What happened?'

'The woman's coat got caught between the closed doors of the train as it left Marble Arch. The driver didn't realize anything was the matter. A customer on the platform saw her being dragged into the tunnel by the departing train.'

Hermione's throat constricted with emotion. 'She must have been frantic with terror.'

'It makes me feel ill just thinking about it,' Angie said. 'The customer had the good sense to tell a member of staff what had happened. The information was then phoned through to the service controller. On his instructions, the traction current was switched off and the train service was suspended between Marble Arch and Liverpool Street.'

'What a terrible way to die.'

'I feel sorry for the station supervisors from Bond Street and Marble Arch.'

'Why?'

Angie said grimly, 'They were asked to search the track between the two Tube stations. The woman's dead body was found about halfway along the tunnel.'

'It's been an unlucky night,' Hermione said. 'First the burst water main outside Pembroke Grove, and now the one under on the Central Line.'

Her instincts told her that Vortex was responsible for the woman's death. She went next door to the kitchen and used her mobile to call the South Lodge at Milsham Castle. But neither Ashley nor Julia Brockman answered, and Hermione rang off with a feeling of unease. The station supervisor remained high on her list of suspects.

She was deliberating what to do next when her mobile rang. Lyle was calling to let her know what had happened at Marble Arch. She heard the horror and outrage in his voice and felt her blood run cold as he described his attempt to save Liz Gillard's life.

'We should never have agreed to get involved in this terrible business,' Hermione said. 'I went along with it because I knew that was what you wanted. You might have been dragged into the tunnel with her.'

Lyle said reassuringly, 'I'm all right. Stop panicking. I'm fine, really.'

Hermione drew her breath in sharply. 'Oh my God, I've just remembered something . . . Darius left here earlier tonight after complaining he was coming down with a migraine.'

'How long ago was this?' Lyle asked sharply.

'It must have been at least an hour ago, maybe longer. I found out he's related to the train driver who was fired for failing his D and A test.'

'Jack Perkins?'

'Who else?' Hermione said grimly. 'They've both got excellent motives for belonging to Vortex.'

All her suspicions of the station control room assistant returned to haunt her. He had turned up late for work, claiming he had got grease on his hand by trying to restart the engine of his broken-down vehicle. But she couldn't help wondering if there was more to it than that. Just where did his uncle — the prophet of doom, as Hermione called him — fit into this business, if at all? She recalled her only encounter with the fired train driver out-side the pub on Tuesday night, and the words he had said: 'Hell is coming sooner than everyone knows!' Were these simply the foolish words of a drunk man, or was there a more sinister meaning behind them?

'Are you attracted to Darius?' Lyle asked suddenly.

'No, of course not,' Hermione said indignantly. 'Whatever gave you a ridicu-lous idea like that?'

'The tone of your voice.'

'Just because I like Darius doesn't mean I'm attracted to him. I happen to like a lot of people, but that doesn't mean anything.' Hermione felt angry with herself for speaking so defensively. She made an effort to speak more calmly. 'For your information, Jacob Adefami visited Pembroke Grove earlier tonight to collect his Santa Claus costume.'

Lyle's voice tightened. 'Are you think-ing what I'm thinking?'

'I'm so overwrought I don't know what to think,' Hermione said irritably. 'He claims he's wearing it to the staff ball tomorrow night.'

'The person who dragged Liz Gillard into the tunnel was dressed in a Santa Claus costume.'

'Are you saying you think Jacob did it?' Hermione gasped.

'I can't be sure. I didn't see the man's face.'

'Where are you now?'

'At Marble Arch Tube Station, assisting the police with their inquiries.'

A shudder passed through Hermione. 'Vortex's violence is spiralling out of control,' she said shakily. 'When is it all going to end?'

★ ★ ★

Lyle slumped back in his chair after he terminated the call on his mobile. He was feeling angry and frightened because he had been unable to prevent Vortex's assassin from escaping on the train.

'I'm sorry I wasn't able to give you a better description of the killer,' he told DS Snare. 'The padded Santa Claus costume suggests he was of medium height and build. This fell out of Liz Gillard's coat pocket and dropped at my feet just before she was dragged into the tunnel.' He pushed a copy of the *Daily Post* across the table to his friend. The front page featured a report on Vortex's deadly activities along with pictures of six of the murdered Tube victims. 'She was convinced she knew the identities of the two men responsible for the Tube murders.'

Nicholas frowned. 'That doesn't get us very far. Are you certain she didn't tell you anything else that could help us crack this case wide open?'

'I'm afraid not.' Lyle moistened his lips and asked, 'What happened after Liz Gillard was dragged to her death inside the tunnel?'

'The killer left the train when it got to Bond Street, took the escalator up to the ticket hall area and disappeared into the street,' Nicholas explained. 'He was caught on the station's CCTV cameras as he left the ticket hall.'

'Did you get a good shot of his face?'

Nicholas shook his head in frustration. 'Have you heard the joke that all men look alike when they're wearing a Santa

Claus costume? In this case it happens to be true. If you don't believe me, here's a print out of the CCTV image.'

Lyle thumped his fist on the desk. 'It's impossible to see his face because he's wearing a hood and beard!' he fumed.

'Lyle, you've got to be careful from now on,' Nicholas warned him. 'Vortex knows you witnessed the murder. The last thing we want is for them to make you their next victim.'

* * *

'Is this your first time travelling in the front cab of a train?' the driver, who answered to the name of J.C., asked in a friendly voice, shortly after the train pulled out of Pembroke Grove Tube Station.

Hermione nodded. 'I was expecting to go home in a taxi tonight,' she said. 'But the street outside Pembroke Grove has been closed by the police because of a burst water main. I'll go with you as far as Paddington Central, then get a taxi from there.'

The latest murder had brought the death toll to seven, and it was apparent to

Hermione that she and Lyle were out of their depth. The murders she had helped him to investigate in the past had been domestic ones; they had no experience of dealing with terrorists. She was convinced the hunt for Vortex ought to be left to the police and the security forces, who had more resources at their disposal.

It had stopped raining a couple of hours ago. But there was still a closeness in the atmosphere; a curious feeling of oppression, almost as if they were waiting for something to happen. In a bid to keep her spirits up, Hermione turned to her companion and asked, 'How long have you been a train driver?'

'Eighteen years.'

'Does it get lonely at times?'

'Some drivers are loners,' J.C. confided. 'I enjoy the company of other people, so I'm always happy to let staff ride with me in my cab. It sharpens my concentration and helps reduce SPADs.'

'What are SPADs?'

'A signal passed at danger. If you have three in a row, your employment is terminated.'

Hermione's eyes widened. 'If a signal is

passed at danger, is it possible for one train to collide with another?'

J.C. shook his head. 'There's no chance of that happening, although the tabloid press often claim we have numerous near-misses. It's all lies, but it sells newspapers. If we come to a signal that's red because it's broken, we don't sit there for ages and wait for someone to come and fix it. We've got a responsibility to the passengers on our train. What happens is that the driver alerts the service controller by radio, who gives permission for the red signal to be passed at danger and for the train to proceed at caution speed to the next station. The tabloid press twists the truth and makes it sound as if we deliberately endanger our passengers' lives.'

'They shouldn't be allowed to get away with telling lies like that,' Hermione remarked.

'It's called telling half-truths,' J.C. said. 'Underneath the train there's a device called a tripcock arm. It's a metal rod that points downwards. When a red signal that's working is passed at danger, the tripcock arm strikes the raised train stop and releases the air from the train's brake-lines. The train automatically stops, and the driver has to reset the tripcock arm before he can proceed.'

'Thank goodness for modern technology,' Hermione murmured.

'When the signal turns green, it lowers the train stop and the train is able to proceed without the tripcock arm being tripped,' J.C. went on. 'SPADs are a driver's worst nightmare.'

'I would have thought a driver's worst nightmare is when a suicidal customer jumps in front of the train,' Hermione said. 'Has that ever happened to you?'

'Only the once,' J.C. said stoically. 'A youth jumped in front of my train four weeks after I qualified as a driver. He was killed outright.'

In the darkness, the train was approaching a brightly lit Tube station. It was Westfield Park. Hermione sensed an unspoken tension emanating from J.C. He was scanning the eastbound platform. Two or three customers were standing well apart from one another, waiting for the incoming train. In the foreground of Westfield Park, silhouetted against the night sky, Hermione saw a bridge eerily lit by street lamps. A vehicle of some sort, possibly a transit van, appeared to have stopped halfway across the bridge.

Moments before they passed under the bridge, there was a loud thud as an unidentified object struck the roof of the driver's cab. Hermione and J.C. exchanged startled glances.

'What was that?' Hermione said.

'Sometimes youths stand on the bridge and throw stones at the windscreen of the driver's cab.'

Hermione's heart was racing. 'The bang was too loud for it to have been stones.'

The train was travelling at thirty miles an hour. The eastbound platform of Westfield Park appeared on their left. J.C. released his pressure on the dead man's handle and the train began cutting speed. This prompted the object on the cab roof to slide forward.

Illuminated by the headlights of the train, the body of a bound and gagged woman with ginger hair, her eyes alive with terror, fell past the windscreen in front of them. Hermione's blood froze as the woman disappeared from sight. There was a sickening thud from beneath the wheels of the train.

'Oh my God — she's fallen onto the electrified rails.'

'Mayday, mayday,' J.C. shouted over the train driver's radio to the service controller. 'This is an emergency. One under — one under ... eastbound Westfield Park ... '

14

The following morning, after taking a shower and getting dressed, Lyle found Hermione sitting in the drawing room of their hotel suite with her knees tucked up under her chin, sipping a cup of much-needed coffee. 'Did you mean what you said last night?' he asked gently.

Hermione threw him a look of reproach. 'Do you really have to ask? We're in over our heads.'

'Hermione, you agreed to get involved in this case.'

'The only reason I'm still here,' she snapped, 'is because I don't want to see you get yourself killed. I'm finding it hard to forget what happened last night. My God, two women were killed before our very eyes! We were powerless to do anything to save them. That's something we're going to have live with for the rest of our lives. My parents are returning from Corsica today. I've half a mind to return to Nettlebed or go and stay with them until this dreadful business is over.'

A note of scorn entered Lyle's voice. 'You're running away because you're frightened.'

Hermione felt her anger mounting. 'Yes, I'm frightened! Does it make you feel better to hear me say it?'

'I'm dammed if I'll lose my nerve and throw in the towel.'

'You're accusing me of being a coward,' Hermione fumed. 'Why don't you admit it?'

Lyle clenched his jaw. 'Is that what running home to your mummy and daddy is all about?'

Hermione flinched. 'What's wrong with wanting to feel safe?'

Lyle threw his hands up in the air. 'How am I supposed to feel safe with Vortex knowing I saw one of their assassins murder Liz Gillard? If you want to run away, Hermione, that's fine by me. I'm not stopping you. I'll even phone for a taxi for you.'

'I can phone for my own taxi — once I've finished packing!' She stormed into their bedroom, opened her suitcase and began flinging clothes into it. She was aware Lyle had followed her, but she was too annoyed and angry to acknowledge his presence.

There was a noticeable pause, then Lyle's voice arrested her actions by saying quietly, 'Have you forgotten how your godmother once survived a Nazi execution squad?'

The question was so unexpected that Hermione stared open-mouthed at him. There was a tense pause, then she slowly shook her head. 'Diana looked fear in the face and confronted it.'

'Hermione, we're not put on this earth to shirk danger and responsibility when they confronts us.'

Hermione's eyes filled with tears. 'All right, then. I'll stay and help you expose Vortex. But only because I couldn't live with myself if anything happened to you. I'm warning you, though, Lyle — this is the last time I'm going to get involved in one of your murder investigations.'

Lyle put his arms around her trembling body and held her close. The arrival of the room service waiter with their breakfast took the edge off their tension. As the waiter left the suite, he passed DS Nicholas Snare in the doorway. The latter looked tired and strained.

'Leona Evans asked me to drop by on my way to work and make sure you're all right after last night's ordeal,' he said. 'She's really sorry you got caught up in it. You'll be pleased to know DI Deveril is under orders to leave the pair of you alone.'

'Have you identified the woman who was killed at Westfield Park?' Hermione asked.

Nicholas nodded and said, 'Her name was Ulrica Corbett-Jones. There was a medical tag around her neck. She was a diabetic. Sometime yesterday afternoon she was abducted from her home.'

Lyle paused with his glass of orange juice halfway to his mouth.

'Abducted from her home?' Hermione repeated bewilderedly.

'I thought you'd be surprised by that,' Nicholas said. 'Ulrica Corbett-Jones lived at Chalfont St Anthony in Sussex. Her husband is understandably distraught. Deveril and I are going down there later today to liaise with the local police.'

'The murders of Liz Gillard and Ulrica Corbett-Jones have shed new light on Vortex's modus operandi,' Lyle remarked thoughtfully. 'There's clearly a considerable degree of calculated method in their madness.'

'Your inner voice isn't wrong there,' Nicholas sighed.

'It's a relief to know we're making progress at last,' Lyle went on. 'Hermione and I hardly got a wink of sleep last night. I found myself flicking through *Every Journey Matters* while I downed a couple of whiskies.' He handed the latest edition of London Underground's in-house magazine to his friend and pointed to a picture. 'Nick, I've been a complete blithering idiot.'

'It's not like you to be so modest.'

'Take a look at the picture of Daniel Fitzpatrick and his wife Sarah attending the LUL Awards for Employee Excellence,' Lyle went on. 'You'll notice she's got red hair.'

'Red hair? What are you talking about?'

Nicholas stared in astonishment at the image.

Lyle's voice rose triumphantly. 'As soon as I saw the picture, I remembered something Peter told me. The Fitzpatricks don't have any children because they've only been married two years. I should have realized sooner that the blonde at the opera was Daniel Fitzpatrick's mistress. Remember how anxious she was to get home because she said she had to get up early to take the boys to school the next morning?'

'It sounds as if Daniel Fitzpatrick is having it off with a married woman,' Nicholas opined. 'She's an attractive bit of goods. I can't say I blame him for having a bit on the side, can you? Would you happen to know the mistress's name?'

'Nick, that's something Hermione and I think you ought to find out for yourself. You might also like to speak to Daniel Fitzpatrick's wife again. Once she knows her husband's got a mistress, she might not be so willing to stand by her statement that he was with her when Fenella Lloyd was murdered.'

'We urgently need a breakthrough in the case,' Nicholas said anxiously. 'Today is Friday, and I've got a nasty feeling Vortex will wreak havoc if their ultimatum isn't met by three o'clock this afternoon.'

*   *   *

Later that morning, DS Nicholas Snare drove past Chalfont St Anthony Railway Station, then took the first turning on the right. Honiton Lane intersected the railway crossing. He and DI Deveril had to wait until the train had passed down the line and the safety barriers were raised before they could continue on their journey.

The secluded residences of Honiton Lane were screened from the road by trees and hedges. The road ascended to the top of a hill. Number 22, an Edwardian house with a garage attached to the side, was the last house on the right. It was currently a crime scene, and the property was cordoned off with police tape. Several police cars were parked by the side of the road.

After finding a suitable parking space,

DI Deveril and DS Snare walked up the driveway. A white-haired man with a dark moustache and an unassuming manner came out of the house and introduced himself in a quietly spoken voice as DI Sutcliffe of the Chalfont St Anthony Constabulary. 'Nasty business,' he said by way of introduction. 'I gather Ulrica Corbett-Jones's body was dropped from a bridge at Westfield Park as the train approached the station.'

'She fell on the tracks and was killed outright,' DI Deveril confirmed.

He was angry with himself for taking the previous night off, especially in light of his discovery that his arch rival Lyle Revel, along with Hermione Bradbury, had taken part in the night's proceedings. He was determined to teach them a lesson they would never forget by exposing Vortex himself.

'The SOCOs are in the living room,' DI Sutcliffe explained. 'We believe that's where the initial attack took place. The front and back doors weren't locked. Anyone could have walked in at any time. The husband came home yesterday evening at five o'clock and found his wife was missing. He immediately contacted the police.'

'Would it be possible to speak to him?' DI Deveril asked.

'Jeremy Corbett-Jones is staying with his parents. The couple live in the house on the opposite side of the road to this one — number nineteen. They were out yesterday afternoon playing bingo, so they didn't see anything.'

While they were speaking, a heavy-set man in a pullover and a pair of jeans had emerged from number nineteen and was crossing the road in a purposeful manner towards them. 'Are you here about Ulrica?' he asked in a deep nasal voice.

DI Sutcliffe said, 'Mr Corbett-Jones, this is DI Deveril and DS Snare from the Metropolitan Police Force in London.'

Beneath his short-cropped tawny hair, Jeremy Corbett-Jones's unshaven face was etched with grief and misery. His broad, fleshy features missed out on being good-looking owing to the width of his nose. The distress in his eyes was so evident that even a man as hard-hearted as DI Deveril felt a stirring of sympathy.

'You've got to find out who did this to Ulrica,' Jeremy Corbett-Jones pleaded. 'He mustn't be allowed to get away with it.'

'We're going to make sure he doesn't,' DI Deveril said in a surprisingly soothing voice. 'Did your wife have any enemies, Mr Corbett-Jones?'

Jeremy Corbett-Jones sat down on the low brick wall bordering the front of the property. He clenched his hands like a distraught child and spoke in a stricken voice. 'It doesn't make sense — any of it.'

DI Deveril adjured himself to remain patient. 'You got home yesterday about five o'clock, I understand?'

'That's right. The garage was empty. Ulrica's transit van should have been there. The dogs were livid at having been left outside in the back garden for so long. Their coats were sodden. I let them inside to dry off in front of the kitchen fire. I knew at once that something wasn't right.'

'How could you know that, sir?'

'The pot of Irish stew on the stove had almost burnt itself dry. Ulrica was proud

257

of her cooking. There's no way she would have gone out like that. Not leaving the dogs outside and cooking on the stove.'

'How long have you been married?'

'Six months.' Jeremy Corbett-Jones's face crumpled with emotion, and for a moment he looked as if he might burst into tears. His words came out in a series of jerks. 'I work in London for a firm of electricians. After I married Ulrica, she gave up her job as a landscape designer. We bought this house and Ulrica set her heart on redecorating it. She'd transformed the garden in the time we lived here.'

'What made you phone the police?' DI Deveril prompted.

'The moment I entered the living room, I knew something was wrong. The cricket bat was lying on the floor. That's what the murdering bastard got her with. There was something red and sticky on the Christmas paper wrapped around it — I touched it and that's when I realized Ulrica's blood was on my fingers.'

DI Sutcliffe murmured, 'Mr Corbett-Jones very sensibly called the police after that.'

They left Jeremy Corbett-Jones siting on the brick wall, overwhelmed with shock, lost in his grief and memories. Having signed the scene of crime register and donned white paper suits, they followed DI Sutcliffe to the living room. The SOCOs were going quietly about their business. There was little in the way of material evidence for DI Deveril and DS Snare to see, but it always helped them both in their investigations to get the layout of a crime scene fixed firmly in their minds.

'Whoever attacked Mrs Corbett-Jones probably hid behind the living room door and struck her from behind,' DI Sutcliffe said. 'There was no evidence of a struggle.' He led the way back down the hall, out through the front door and to the garage by the side of the house. 'The garage doors were found open,' he added. 'The white transit van belonging to Mrs Corbett-Jones was missing. The husband says there's an Axminster rug missing from the living room. It was probably wrapped around her body. If anyone saw the killer taking it out to the transit van, they would have had no reason to assume there was a body rolled up inside it.'

DI Deveril asked, 'Have any witnesses come forward?'

DI Sutcliffe shook his head. 'No, it's a secluded lane. Very quiet and peaceful under normal circumstances.'

'As you know from our phone conversation,' DS Snare said, 'the white transit van was seen on the bridge moments before the body was dropped onto the track at Westfield Park. The transit van was abandoned several streets away after it broke down. Whoever stole it attempted to restart the engine without success. An Axminster rug was found in the back of the vehicle. Why did she have a transit van?'

'Prior to her marriage, she worked for a landscape gardening firm in London. She hadn't got round to selling it. She found it useful to have for visiting the local nursery and buying plants and statues for the garden.'

'When was Ulrica Corbett-Jones last seen alive?'

'Three o'clock. A neighbour saw her

getting the mail from her letter box and going back inside the house.'

'The husband got home at five o'clock,' DS Nicholas Snare recalled. 'That gives us a two-hour window between three o'clock and five o'clock when Vortex abducted Mrs Corbett-Jones. It would have taken around an hour to drive her unconscious body up to London.' He made a mental note to pass the information on to Lyle Revel, then added thoughtfully, 'Whoever killed her went to a lot of trouble to abduct her first.'

15

Assistant Commissioner Leona Evans entered DI Deveril's office. 'What's this I hear about you bringing Daniel Fitzpatrick in for questioning again?' she demanded.

DI Deveril was not averse to taking false credit for a break-through in a case in order to further his own career. 'At my suggestion, DS Snare phoned Sarah Fitzpatrick earlier this afternoon at her sister's home in Cambridge. She's retracted her statement. Now she claims her husband wasn't with her at all on Friday evening. Daniel Fitzpatrick doesn't have an alibi for the time of Fenella Lloyd's murder.'

Leona Evans nodded approvingly. 'Anything else?'

DI Deveril was preening himself. His former self-doubts about solving the case had evaporated now that Daniel Fitzpatrick was in police custody. He was convinced the slimy two-faced son of a bitch was the controlling force behind

Vortex. It was a well-known fact that the deputy managing director of London Underground was opposed to privatization. With any luck, it wouldn't be long before Daniel Fitzpatrick confessed. Once he was convicted of the Tube murders, Deveril's promotion to chief inspector would be assured.

'Sarah Fitzpatrick also alleges a black burka and veil have gone missing from the Fitzpatrick residence.'

'Get a search warrant,' Leona Evans said crisply. 'I want the Fitzpatrick property gone over from top to bottom.'

'The property is being searched as we speak, ma'am. A search of the perimeter has established there's a small door in a brick wall at the rear. The door appears to belong to the neighbouring property when, in fact, it provides access to the Fitzpatrick residence. It would have been entirely possible for Daniel Fitzpatrick to come and go over the last few days without our surveillance officers knowing.'

★　★　★

The central heating was not working properly, and the atmosphere in interview room number two was as chilly as the room itself.

'Why should I believe a word you've told me?' DI Deveril demanded.

'I've told you the truth,' Daniel Fitzpatrick said earnestly. 'When Fenella Lloyd was being murdered on Friday evening, I was at home with my wife Sarah.'

'Your wife has changed her story.'

Fitzpatrick appeared to be in the grip of a strong emotion. He took a deep breath before speaking again.

'Sarah is only saying that because she's upset to learn about my affair with Vanessa Zellweger.'

'Can you blame your wife for being angry?'

'She's doing this to spite me.'

DI Deveril was convinced the suspect was guilty. 'What happened to the black burka and veil Mrs Fitzpatrick bought her niece to wear in a school play?'

Fitzpatrick groaned. 'The idea of a niece of mine dressing up and pretending to be a Muslim woman struck me as disrespectful. It made me angry. It was rather rash of me, but I threw the burka and veil out.'

'Without telling your wife?'

The sneering contempt in DI Deveril's voice made Fitzpatrick wilt inside his expensive suit. 'At the time, I wanted to avoid an argument with my wife,' he replied in a self-consciously brittle voice.

'You must have known there would be one hell of a row when she found out, Mr Fitzpatrick.' DI Deveril smiled ferociously and leaned across the interview table. 'Are you sure you didn't wear the black burka and veil as a disguise when you pushed Norwood Mackintosh under the train at Covent Garden?'

Fitzpatrick flinched. 'I did nothing of the sort!'

'The CCTV footage shows a figure in a black burka and veil passing behind Norwood Mackintosh seconds before he stumbled and fell under the train. You deliberately tripped him. He was murdered along with all your previous victims.'

'Someone else committed those murders,' Fitzpatrick insisted. 'The board of

London Underground has suspended me pending the outcome of the police investigation into the Tube murders. I was home alone getting drunk when Norwood Mackintosh was murdered. Sarah had gone to Cambridge to spend Christmas with her family.'

DI Deveril gave a snide laugh. 'Attempting to drown your demons, were you?'

'Do you seriously think I tried to kill Fenella Lloyd at Piccadilly Circus without the benefit of a disguise?'

DI Deveril was unimpressed by the suspect's logic. 'Maybe your encounter with her was accidental.'

'Of course it was,' Fitzpatrick said impatiently. 'I tripped on my untied shoelace and stumbled against her. You haven't given me a single credible reason why I should murder eight people.'

'You want Peter Hamilton's job,' DI Deveril said bluntly. 'Ever since he came over from America and robbed you of your rightful promotion, you've been festering inside.'

'This is pure speculation.'

'You keep looking at your watch, Mr

Fitzpatrick,' DI Deveril remarked. 'Three o'clock has come and gone. You must be wondering if London Underground has given in to Vortex's ultimatum, got rid of Peter Hamilton and made you their new managing director.'

'Nonsense!'

'Why don't you admit you disapprove of Peter Hamilton's stance on privatization?'

'So do a lot of people!' Fitzpatrick snapped. 'I'd make a better leader than him any day! As managing director of London Underground, I'd cancel plans to privatize the Tube with immediate effect. There'd be no more murders.'

'How can you possibly know that,' DI Deveril demanded, 'unless you're behind all the murders that have been committed?'

Aware that he had said too much, Fitzpatrick retreated into silence.

'You hate Peter Hamilton and everything he stands for, including privatization. You even hate the fact he had a beautiful ex-wife in Fenella Lloyd. I think you're the controlling force behind Vortex.'

Fitzpatrick drew himself up to his full height. 'I'm not that big a fool.'

'Do you know what I think happened, Mr Fitzpatrick? By chance you encountered Fenella Lloyd at Piccadilly Circus two days before she was murdered. Subconsciously you wanted her dead, but you couldn't bring yourself to admit as much to yourself. That's why you persuaded yourself afterwards that you'd stumbled accidentally against her.'

'Nonsense!'

'The desire to kill became stronger. After confronting the evil in your heart, you donned a black burka and veil. Your next attempt on Fenella's life, this time at Leicester Square, was entirely successful.'

'No, you've got it all wrong.'

DI Deveril's voice rang out sharply. 'Where did you go last night?'

'What makes you think I went anywhere?'

'We've had you under police surveillance for several days. You left your house dressed in a Santa Claus costume. The CCTV footage from Holland Park Tube Station shows you entering the ticket hall at 10:32 p.m. You boarded the same train on which Liz Gillard was travelling to work. When she got off at Marble Arch Tube Station, you grabbed hold of her coat as the doors of the departing train shut and dragged her to her death inside the tunnel.'

Fitzpatrick broke out into a cold sweat. 'I did nothing of the sort! You're entirely mistaken.'

'After the train got to Bond Street Tube Station, you were caught on camera leaving the station through the ticket hall.'

Fitzpatrick loosened his tie. 'I — I admit I was wearing a Santa Claus costume and that I entered Holland Park Tube Station at the time you say I did. But I got off one stop later at Notting Hill Gate. I didn't go as far as Marble Arch.'

'What possible reason could you have for getting off at Notting Hill Gate, Mr Fitzpatrick?'

'Vanessa Zellweger rang me to say her husband was away. She asked me to come round to her house dressed as Santa Claus and give her two boys a sack of presents.'

'How old are they?'

'Five and six.' Fitzpatrick appeared to have regained some of his poise. 'The idea was for the boys to put the presents under their Christmas tree and open them on Christmas day.'

'Do you seriously expect me to believe this farrago of nonsense?'

'Vanessa has been hinting for some time that I'm the father of the youngest boy, Alex, and I thought it only right I should meet him. I rather suspect she wants me to divorce my wife. My marriage to Sarah was a mistake, and if the opportunity to marry Vanessa arose I'd jump at it. I rather think she feels the same way.'

'What happened to prevent you from reaching Vanessa Zellweger's house? Did you eye Liz Gillard up on the train and decide to make her your next victim?'

Fitzpatrick flushed. 'When I got to Vanessa's house, I saw her husband's car parked outside. It was obvious he'd come home early from his overseas business trip. It was a damn nuisance. But there was nothing I could do about it. In fact, I felt bloody put out. I walked home — '

'Rather than take the Tube?'

'Normally I go for a walk each night just before I turn in. Last night was no exception. I needed to clear my thoughts.'

'I don't believe a word you're telling me. After killing Liz Gillard, you went to Westfield Park and dropped Ulrica Corbett-Jones's body from the bridge.'

Fitzpatrick struggled to remain calm. 'I did nothing of the sort!'

'Will Vanessa Zellweger be able to verify any part of your story?'

'Well, hardly,' Fitzpatrick protested. 'How could she? Her husband would have become suspicious if I'd turned up on the doorstep.'

'You're lying,' DI Deveril sneered. 'Why don't you admit you killed Liz Gillard and left the train at Bond Street? We've got images from the CCTV footage showing you leaving the station through the ticket hall.'

Fitzpatrick moistened his lips. 'It's not beyond the realms of possibility that another person in a Santa Claus costume was on the same train as Liz Gillard,' he said. 'Volunteers from St Barnaby's Hospice are doing their annual fundraising at Tube stations in central London. They're all wearing Santa Claus costumes.'

DI Deveril gave a slow, cruel smile. 'So you admit to being on the same train as Liz Gillard?'

'I'm innocent, I tell you.'

'In that case, Mr Fitzpatrick, why did you burn the Santa Claus costume in the incinerator in your back garden?'

Daniel Fitzpatrick's voice rose in desperation. 'It was on the news this morning that someone wearing a Santa Claus costume had killed a woman at Marble Arch by dragging her into the tunnel. I didn't want people to think it was me. I panicked and lost my nerve. But contrary to what you're thinking, I'm not in league with Vortex. I don't know who's killing our customers.'

★ ★ ★

The first of Hermione's and Lyle's guests arrived at Claridge's shortly before four o'clock. Sinead O'Leary's face was red and she was breathing hard.

'I've just walked all the way from Marble Arch. There was no way I was going to take the Tube — not after what happened to my Reggie.'

'You sound upset,' Lyle said. 'What's the matter?'

'Have you seen this afternoon's edition of the *Evening Herald*? London Underground has refused to call off privatization.'

'Hermione and I have already heard the news. It was to be expected, I'm afraid.'

'You know what's going to happen now that Vortex's ultimatum has been ignored, don't you?' Sinead said. 'Vortex will go on killing innocent people until they get their way.'

'I think you're probably right. By the way, I'd like you to meet Hermione.'

'I was sorry to hear about your loss,' Hermione said gently. 'Lyle and I are also anxious to see Vortex's activities curtailed.'

Sinead's eyes flashed with anger. 'London Underground should have given into Vortex's demands and called off privatization.'

'The government and London Underground can't submit to Vortex,' Lyle said.

'If they did, it would only encourage other terrorist groups to hold them to ransom.'

Peter Hamilton arrived ten minutes later, looking surprisingly determined and resolute despite the pressure he was under as managing director of London Underground. Once Lyle had made the necessary introductions, Sinead came directly to the point.

'How could you refuse to cancel privatization? Eight commuters are already dead. Vortex is planning to go on killing more innocent people. Do you even have a conscience?'

'I understand only too well how you're feeling,' Peter replied. 'In order to ensure Vortex is caught, I've elicited the help of Lyle and Hermione, who have a proven track record as crime solvers.'

Sinead stared at the couple in surprise. 'Why did no one tell me this before?'

'Careless talk costs lives,' Lyle replied. 'Hermione and I have successfully investigated a number of cases in the past. Rest assured, Sinead, we're going to do all that is necessary to bring Vortex to justice.

Adrian Knowles arrived then, looking pale and shaken by recent events. Any animosity the bookshop owner and Peter Hamilton felt towards each other at having been rivals in love for the same woman was held firmly in check. Hermione introduced Sinead and Adrian to each other, and it was apparent at once that Sinead felt she had found a kindred spirit in the unhappy young man.

'Vortex is every bit as devious as the IRA once were,' Sinead said. 'Reggie might not have been special to anyone else. But he was mine and all I had. Now that Vortex has gone and taken him away from me, I'll never forgive them.'

'I know how you feel,' Adrian said with a tremor in his voice. 'Fenella and I were hoping to get married and go to India for our honeymoon — only now . . . ' He broke off, unable to go on.

'Only now you're facing the future alone like me.' Sinead laid a tender hand on his arm and turned to Peter. 'My brother has helped me to set up a website. It's called United Against Vortex. Over a hundred and fifty thousand members of the public have signed up to it. I've been overwhelmed by messages of condolence and support.'

'You'll be interested to know London Underground will be holding a memorial service in the New Year for the family and friends of all the victims.'

Peter's announcement was met with a general murmur of approval.

'The reason Lyle and Hermione have invited us here today,' he added, 'is because they have something they want to say to us.'

Lyle said, 'Ulrica Corbett-Jones was abducted from her home before her body was thrown onto the track at Westfield Park. Her murder indicates Vortex has been carefully pre-selecting its victims.'

'But I don't see why,' Sinead said bewilderedly.

'Nor do we,' Hermione said. 'That's why we need your help. Last night Lyle had the misfortune to witness the murder of Liz Gillard at Marble Arch.'

Lyle went on, 'Before she died, she said, 'I know why these people are being pushed in front of the trains. It's come to me just now . . . The man who's doing this is out to get us all — I always said he and the other man were wrong 'uns.''

There was a stunned silence as everyone absorbed the enormity of the dead woman's words.

'She must have known who the members of Vortex are,' Sinead said, frowning. 'That would explain why she was killed.'

'But I don't see how she could have known,' Adrian objected. 'Who are the two men, and why did she think they were out to get everyone?'

The conversation was cut short by the arrival of the room service waiter who entered the suite with a trolley on which afternoon tea was laid out. Tea was poured, and they sat around reminiscing about their loved ones.

'Reggie's real name was Reginald O'Rourke,' Sinead said. 'He changed his surname because he wanted to be an actor. One of the most exciting times in his life was when he was called up to do jury work. He was hoping to be chosen as the foreperson of the jury. But the other jurors picked a woman instead.'

'Fenella was once a foreperson on a jury,' Peter said with an air of surprised recollection.

'How long ago was this?' Adrian asked curiously.

Peter frowned. 'About a year ago, I think.'

'Reggie also did his jury service around that time,' Sinead said. 'I wonder if he and Fenella were on the same jury together?'

'Isn't that a rather far-fetched idea?' Adrian asked.

'Reggie and I met for the first time in April this year,' Sinead said. 'He later mentioned he was once on a jury that found two robbers guilty of murder at the Old Bailey.'

'Fenella also sat on a jury at the Old Bailey,' Peter confirmed. 'I don't know anything else about the case because she was under oath not to talk about it. I imagine the two men went to prison for a long time.'

Lyle suddenly felt as if an electric charge had gone through him. He left the others talking in the sitting room and went next door to the bedroom. He rang DS Nicholas Snare's mobile number.

'Nick, Vortex has been leading everyone up the garden path. They've made complete fools of us all.'

'You're not making much sense.'

Lyle's voice rose excitedly. 'I've just discovered Fenella Lloyd and Reggie Dalloway did jury service at the Old Bailey a year ago.'

'Are you telling me they were on the same jury?' Nicholas demanded.

'I'm almost certain of it,' Lyle said triumphantly.

'What reason could Vortex have for bumping off the members of a jury?' Nicholas asked quickly.

'Revenge is a powerful motive,' Lyle said. 'One or more of Vortex's members must be related to the two defendants who were found guilty of robbery and murder. So far Vortex has killed eight members of the public.'

'A jury is made up of twelve people.'

'Leaving four jurors still unaccounted for,' Lyle agreed.

Nicholas's voice rang out incredulously. 'My God, are you saying four more people are going to be murdered on London Underground?'

'That's exactly what I'm saying,' Lyle said urgently. 'It looks as if Vortex is killing the jury off, one by one.'

16

Assistant Commissioner Leona Evans was white-faced with shock. She was standing in DI Deveril's office, staring at the list of names on the sheet of paper he had just given her.

'Are you telling me the eight Tube victims served together on a jury at the Old Bailey?' she snapped.

'Yes.'

'Why didn't you find out sooner by running a check on the victims through the Police National Computer?'

'Someone hacked into the system and made it crash a fortnight ago.'

Leona Evans flushed. The computer system's shut-down had completely slipped her memory. She hated it when Deveril got one up on her.

'Our hacker is a fourteen-year-old teenager living in Salt Lake City in America,' DI Deveril continued. 'The FBI has also confirmed he successfully hacked into the

Pentagon, causing a 21-day shutdown of their computer system.'

Leona Evans stared at him. 'You're telling me our investigation into the Underground murders has been jeopardized by a fourteen-year-old?'

'That's the size of it, ma'am. Operation Piranha has been successful in getting the Police National Computer up and running. It's been back online for the last two hours. The remaining four jurors are still alive. Once they're found and taken into protective custody, everything will be fine.'

DS Snare entered the office. He was breathing hard. 'Ma'am, our officers have gone round to the homes of the four jurors. We've drawn a complete blank.'

'What do you mean?'

'All four appear to be missing.'

Leona Evans consulted the list in her hand. 'What about Carly Pringle?'

'Her employer Gala Theatre Tickets has given her several days off over the Christmas period. Normally she works at the theatre desk at Claridge's. She's gone to Essex to stay with some friends. No one knows their names or address.'

'Ophelia Ogden?'

DS Snare said apprehensively, 'She hasn't been seen at her home in Ealing Broadway for over a week. No one knows where she is.'

Leona Evans lifted her gaze from the list in her hand. 'Jeremy Corbett-Jones?'

'He's been very depressed since his wife Ulrica was murdered. His parents are deeply worried. He went missing from their home earlier today.'

'It defies belief that a husband and wife could be called up to serve on the same jury,' DI Deveril muttered. 'They must have met first as jurors, fallen in love afterwards and married.'

'And the fourth remaining juror, Vasilis Demetrious?' Leona Evans rapped.

'Apparently Vasilis Demetrious is at work, ma'am.'

Leona Evans' voice was icily calm. 'Have you contacted his employer?'

DS Snare nodded. 'I've already spoken to Peter Hamilton. Vasilis Demetrious is a train driver for London Underground.'

An hour earlier, in the darkness of the overheated train driver's cab, the voice of the service controller came over the radio. 'Service controller to train 205. Do you receive?'

Vasilis Demetrious had a bullet-shaped head and a heavy five o'clock shadow. Although he had been a UK resident for eighteen years, he spoke in a deep voice that still bore traces of a Greek accent. 'Train 205 receiving. State your message.'

'Hammersmith station is closed because of defective platform lighting. I want you to tip out your train at Goldhawk Road and travel empty to Hammersmith.'

In accordance with LUL radio procedure, Vasilis repeated back over the radio the instructions he had been given.

'Affirmative,' the service controller said. 'Hammersmith station will probably be closed for the rest of the night. Trains will continue to run as booked on the Hammersmith and City Line. All westbound trains departing from Hammersmith will enter passenger service at Goldhawk Road, and all eastbound trains like yourself will tip out at Goldhawk Road and run empty to Hammersmith.'

Vasilis acknowledged the radio message. His train was currently stationary on the westbound platform at Shepherd's Bush Market. The Tube station was situated on an open section of track known as the Hammersmith and City branch line, and the darkness of the fog-shrouded night was punctuated by the dimly glowing lights of suburbia.

The opo monitors inside Vasilis's cab indicated the platform was clear. He pushed a button that closed the passenger doors on the westbound side of the train. With a deftness born of ten years' experience, he applied pressure to the dead man's handle. The train glided out of Shepherd's Bush Market Tube Station. It was a freezing cold Friday night. A thick fog lay over London, obscuring objects and buildings, giving them a surreal, slightly nightmarish quality. He would be glad when his shift was over.

Vasilis looked at his companion, who was dressed in a London Underground uniform, and said with a weary shake of his head, 'The passengers aren't going to enjoy being asked to leave the train at Goldhawk Road.'

'I can't say I blame them on a night as cold as this. I'm glad I'm travelling part of the way home in the warmth of your cab.'

'Winter is the time of the year I hate most,' Vasilis said with a grin. 'You should see my electricity bill. My wife Delia has every heater turned on in our house.' He chuckled to himself, full of adoration for his wife. 'Even when she goes to bed at night, she leaves the heaters turned on full blast! Her favourite time of the year is Christmas. That's because she loves cooking. She can cook anything to perfection.'

'Your figure is proof of that.'

Vasilis looked down at his large stomach and chuckled again. 'That's what everyone tells me. Ours is the perfect marriage. Always I tell Delia that. She loves cooking and I love eating. Last year we had a terrible disaster. Delia forgot to defrost the turkey in time. She spent the whole of Christmas day sobbing her eyes out.'

Less than a minute later, the train

glided into Goldhawk Road Tube Station and stopped alongside the westbound platform. He pushed a button that opened all the passenger doors on the westbound side of the train.

Vasilis addressed the passengers over the train tannoy system. 'Ladies and gents, this train terminates here. Hammersmith station is closed because of defective platform lighting. Could everyone please leave the train now? Bus 295 or 220 outside this station will take you to Hammersmith.'

The disgruntled passengers were slow to respond. At the rear end of the westbound platform, a burly station assistant came up the stairs to assist with the detrainment. Once the train was empty and ready to proceed, he gave the right of way by raising his hand above his head. Vasilis pressed down on the dead man's handle and the train drew out of the station. The train glided five hundred metres down the track, then stopped as they came to a red signal.

Vasilis looked at his passenger and shook his head in a befuddled manner.

'Delia is always saying I've got a terrible memory for names and faces. I hope you weren't offended by my not remembering who you are.'

Vasilis drew his ringing mobile out of his pocket and answered the call. 'Delia, I haven't forgotten. I'm in the front cab of my train, just outside Hammersmith. In another ten minutes' time I'll be booking off duty. I promise I'll stop off at the Broadway Shopping Centre and get the cranberry sauce for the turkey. I can't stay on my mobile talking to you because I've got a member of staff with me from Pembroke Grove station.' Vasilis spoke to his wife for another minute or two, then he terminated the call. He took his thermos from the dashboard and dropped it into his bag, which was lying on the floor next to his seat.

Suddenly the killer's black-gloved hand lashed out, stabbing Vasilis in the back of the neck with a knife. He grunted in agony and then fell to the floor in an unconscious heap, blood oozing from the wound.

There were four doors in a train

driver's cab — the J door leading to the carriage behind, the K and L doors on the left and right sides of the train, and the M door at the front of the cab. It was easy for the killer to open the L door and shove Vasilis's body onto the electrified eastbound tracks that were adjacent to the westbound tracks on which the stationary train was standing. Vasilis was immediately electrocuted.

The signal turned green. The killer shut the L door, switched off the light in the cab and pressed down on the dead man's handle.

It was precisely eight p.m. when train 205 glided into Hammersmith and berthed effortlessly alongside platform three. The station was shrouded in darkness. Fog obscured the lenses of the CCTV cameras. There were no signs of any staff on duty. The freezing weather had driven them indoors.

Unobserved, the killer left the deserted station and disappeared into the crowd of Christmas shoppers outside in the street.

⋆　⋆　⋆

289

On Saturday morning, Lyle Revel woke from an enjoyable dream and reached out to make love to Hermione. But before he could do so, he was distracted by the buzzing of his mobile alerting him to the arrival of a text message.

DS Nicholas Snare's missive read: 'Vortex is killing the jurors in the Kevin Brockman murder case. Suggest you speak to Hermione's uncle Sir Roland Anstruther and let me know how you get on.'

'Who's Kevin Brockman?' Lyle said, showing the text message to Hermione.

'I wouldn't be at all surprised if he's related to Ashley and Julia Brockman,' she exclaimed.

'Who as we both know are the worst caretakers Milsham Castle has ever had,' Lyle said before she could utter her well-worn phrase. 'I told you all along that they were hiding something from us.'

Hermione and Lyle looked at each other and grinned. The strain they had been under was replaced by a surge of adrenaline.

'This is the best eureka moment we've

had all week,' she said, hugging him enthusiastically. 'I can't help feeling the end of case is in sight.'

Following a series of phone calls, they got hold of Sir Roland Anstruther, who was working overtime that morning at Gray's Inn. Shortly after midday, the couple found themselves sitting opposite the barrister in his elegantly furnished chambers.

'As I mentioned on the phone to you, the Hatton Garden robbery attracted enormous publicity,' Sir Roland recalled in his rich, fruity voice. 'The two co-defendants charged with killing the security guard were Kevin Brockman and Ben Skinner. Each day Kevin's parents Ashley and Julia Brockman sat in the public gallery listening to the proceedings. The trial lasted four weeks owing to the complexity of the evidence. It was a relief when it was finally over.'

Hermione was unable to contain herself any longer. 'Uncle Roly, tell us what happened,' she said impatiently.

'In May of last year, Kevin Brockman and Ben Skinner rode up to Chevalier's on a motorbike. Brockman entered the store armed with a pistol and ordered the terrified staff to fill a bag with jewellery. He then locked them inside a broom cupboard at the back of the store. It was the security guard's tragedy to return early from his lunch break. Tommy Tingwell tackled Brockman as he was leaving the store. Ben Skinner, who was acting as a lookout, leapt off his motorbike and raced inside to help him. In the struggle that ensued, Tommy Tingwell was shot dead by one of them.'

'Did Ben Skinner also have a pistol?'

Sir Roland shook his head. 'Only Brockman was armed. Later in court, both men accused each other of firing the fatal shot that killed Tommy Tingwell.'

'I'm surprised the security cameras didn't capture what happened,' Hermione remarked.

'There was a blind spot behind the jewellery counter,' Sir Roland said wistfully. 'Brockman and Skinner took off with over two hundred and fifty thousand pounds' worth of stolen jewellery. Five days later, a member of the public rang the police after seeing the two fugitives near a cottage owned by Brockman on the Dorset coast. It was later found to be filled with loot from four other robberies committed by the pair.

'The police surrounded the cottage. We'll never know for certain whether Brockman or Skinner opened fire on the police. Brockman later insisted my client instigated the attack. But Ben Skinner was equally adamant that he woke up halfway through the shoot-out and only returned fire on the police because he feared for his life. Three police officers were shot and injured before Brockman and Skinner were overpowered and arrested.'

'I bet that didn't go down well with the judge,' Hermione said.

'It certainly made my job of defending Ben Skinner more difficult,' Sir Roland said gravely. 'Prior to the trial, I visited him in the holding cells beneath the Old Bailey. He begged me to believe he was innocent. Despite being an experienced barrister, I couldn't help wanting to believe him, although I knew there was a distinct possibility he was lying to me. On the first morning of the trial, Ben Skinner broke down uncontrollably and sobbed his eyes out in the dock. By the second day he seemed transformed, as if he'd finally had the confidence to believe I could successfully defend him. It was a pity in a way. He came across as a little too cocky in the witness box. Kevin Brockman made a better impression and fared better under cross-examination.'

Lyle said, 'What was Kevin Brockman's response when the verdict of guilty was read out?'

A note of grim satisfaction entered Sir Roland's voice. 'The roar of approbation from the public gallery upset Brockman a great deal. My client, on the other hand, wept like an abandoned child. I was as shocked as everyone else when Brockman began punching Ben Skinner in the head and accusing him of murdering the security guard. Somehow I don't think the jury or anyone else was fooled by Brockman's shallow subterfuge. His mask was pulled back to reveal the vicious animal underneath.'

Hermione said, 'How did Ashley and

Julia Brockman react when their son was found guilty of murder?'

Sir Roland smiled. 'I thought you might ask me that. Julia had an attack of panic and screamed at the jury, 'Kevin is innocent! How could you do this to him?' She then fainted and had to be removed from the court.'

'I can't say I'm surprised by her reaction,' Hermione said. 'Julia Brockman is the clinging, neurotic type. Women like that invariably have a strong maternal streak.'

Lyle said, 'How did Ben Skinner's family react to the guilty verdict?'

'Ben Skinner was orphaned at the age of four,' Sir Roland replied. 'His formative years were spent being looked after by a succession of foster parents. At the age of twelve he raped his eleven-year-old sister Jo. The authorities sent Jo to live with a Scottish couple who adopted her. Owing to the trauma Jo endured, she slit her wrists and never saw her brother again.'

'Oh my God.' Hermione was horrified.

'Ben Skinner was sent to live with a

new set of foster parents in London's East End. As a young man, he developed a reputation for beating up his girlfriends. He clearly wasn't the sort of man any parent would want their daughter to take up with. Shortly before the trial, he narrowly avoided being charged with raping a forty-six-year-old woman.'

'What a vicious creep.'

Sir Roland nodded in agreement with his niece's sentiments. 'Initially I was fooled by Ben Skinner's little-boy-lost act,' he confessed. 'He got no more than he deserved when he was convicted of Tommy Tingwell's murder. But I doubt if we'll ever know if it was his hand or Kevin Brockman's that fired the fatal shot that ended Tommy Tingwell's life.'

'When are they due to be released from prison?'

Sir Roland stared at Lyle in surprise and said, 'In February this year, Ben Skinner got into a fight with an inmate at Brixton Prison. The inmate slit his throat.'

'Uncle Roly, are you saying Ben Skinner is dead?'

'Very much so,' Sir Roland said. 'No

one attended his funeral. He died intestate. A most unsavoury character. I'm sorry I ever defended him.'

'What about Kevin Brockman?' Lyle asked quickly.

'Kevin Brockman was one of nine inmates who died a month ago when a fire raged through the east wing of Risely Vale Prison. The fire was caused when an oil tanker crashed off the road and exploded against the side of the prison.'

Lyle and Hermione were shocked by these unexpected events. It took them several moments to readjust their ideas.

'Uncle Roly, what you've told us throws a completely different light on the case.' Hermione gazed bewilderedly at Lyle. 'Just before Liz Gillard was killed at Marble Arch, she told you she knew who was responsible for the Tube murders.'

'She can't have known Kevin Brockman and Ben Skinner are dead,' Lyle said thoughtfully.

'On the other hand, Ashley and Julia Brockman are very much alive,' Hermione reminded him. 'What's more, they have an excellent motive for killing the jury. Julia is a neurotic and vindictive woman who might easily follow her husband's lead and get caught up in murder.'

'They're going to have a lot of explaining to do when the police catch up with them,' Sir Roland opined.

Hermione turned to her uncle. 'After I heard about the one under at Marble Arch, I immediately phoned the South Lodge to see if Ashley Brockman was home. But no one took my call. Mrs Elliott visited the South Lodge for me earlier this morning. The Brockmans appear to be missing.'

'It looks as if the birds have flown,' Lyle said.

'Have you any idea where they might be?' Sir Roland asked.

Hermione shook her head. 'The couple are planning to move into a flat in Bayswater, but it's not available until the New Year. Ashley has a week off work. He isn't due to return to Pembroke Grove until next Thursday. It's possible he and Julia might have gone away together for a short weekend break. But I find that difficult to believe.'

'So do I, since the couple are still struggling to pay off the legal costs of their son's trial,' Sir Roland said. 'That would explain why they also got a job working for Lord Milsham. I imagine it's going to take them a considerable amount of time to get back on their feet financially.'

Hermione shivered. 'Only three jurors are still alive. I've got a horrible feeling they're all going to die as part of Vortex's sick game.'

'For some inexplicable reason,' Sir Roland said gravely, 'this terrible business reminds me of Haydn's *Farewell Symphony*, where portions of the orchestra steal away towards the end — one by one — until the stage is left completely empty.'

★   ★   ★

Jeremy Corbett-Jones was standing on the bridge at Westfield Park, shivering in the cold Saturday night air. The world seemed a terrifying place without Ulrica by his side. The bright future they had planned together was gone forever.

Memories were such cruel things. He desperately longed to be with Ulrica — to hear the sound of her voice and laughter, to savour the warmth of her body pressed against his, to feel the softness of her breath on his cheek. But she was dead — taken from him by a callous terrorist group with no respect for life.

Jeremy's parents had done their best to shield him from the pain of Ulrica's murder. They had insisted on identifying her body for the police. 'It's best you remember Ulrica the way she was,' his father had told him, 'rather than how she ended up, son.'

Yesterday, without telling his parents where he was going or what he was doing, Jeremy had taken their car and driven up to London. Since his arrival in the capital, he had visited places that had been special to Ulrica and him — Regent's Park, the Tate Gallery, their favourite bookshop and restaurant.

Jeremy had at last summoned the courage to come to the bridge from which

Vortex had thrown Ulrica's body. In his hands was a bunch of roses and lilies — Ulrica's favourite flowers. Below him was the electrified railway line on which she had died. In the distance he could see an eastbound train making its way towards him.

Jeremy's eyes were reddened and his lungs were exhausted from prolonged weeping. He should have known from the beginning that their love for each other was cursed. After all, they'd met on the same jury that had found the two robbers guilty of the murder of the security guard.

Jeremy was about to drop the flowers on to the railway track in honour of Ulrica's memory when his mobile rang. The insistent ringing stirred an improbable fantasy in him. Ulrica was trying to get through to him to let him know she was alive — there'd been a terrible mistake; a case of mistaken identity . . .

'Hello?'

DS Snare's voice sounded in his ear. 'Mr Corbett-Jones, this is Detective Sergeant Snare.'

At once Jeremy's hopes faded like a star

falling to earth. 'Yes, what do you want?' he croaked.

'You're in terrible danger. Vortex is killing the jury on which you and your wife served in the Skinner and Brockman case.'

In the incident room at police head-quarters in central London, DS Nicholas Snare leapt up from his desk, urging himself to speak calmly into the phone. 'Where are you now, Mr Corbett-Jones?'

'I'm standing on the bridge in front of Westfield Park Tube Station.'

Seconds later, DS Nicholas Snare heard an agonised scream of pain as the killer drove a knife into the back of Jeremy Corbett-Jones's neck.

17

'Are you telling me Jeremy Corbett-Jones is dead?' Assistant Commissioner Leona Evans demanded the following morning.

'That's right, ma'am,' DI Deveril said grimly. 'Last night Vortex threw his body from the bridge at Westfield Park in front of an incoming train. His murder has chilling echoes of his wife Ulrica's.'

White-faced with apprehension, Leona Evans said, 'There are only two jurors left.'

That afternoon, Sunday 23rd December, Peter Hamilton chaired an emergency board meeting of the directors of London Underground at 55 Broadway. The company was facing its biggest crisis in years and the atmosphere was rife with nervous tension.

'We can't afford to underestimate the severity of the situation,' Stan Ericson-Monroe was saying anxiously. 'Or the threat posed by Vortex.'

The conversation broke off in mid-sentence as Peter's work mobile rang. He pressed a buzzer on the table and two police protection officers immediately entered the board room. Peter transferred the call to speaker-phone. 'Peter Hamilton speaking.'

A man's rasping voice said, 'It's a pity you didn't see Ulrica Corbett-Jones die. The sound of her screams reminded me of a pig having its throat slit. Last night I got an even bigger thrill pushing her husband off the bridge at Westfield Park. I also killed one of your train drivers on Friday night.'

'Vasilis Demetrious was a member of the RMT,' Peter cried angrily. 'Why in God's name did you have to kill him?'

'Anyone who gets in Vortex's way can expect to be eliminated. Vortex is extending its deadline. You've got until midday on Monday to carry out our instructions.'

Peter broke out into a cold sweat. 'I'm damned if I'll appoint Daniel Fitzpatrick as my successor and resign as managing director. Do you seriously think the British government is going to be bullied into submission by Vortex?'

The anonymous caller's next words horrified everyone. 'Just to prove Vortex means business, we're going to let a runaway train loose on the Piccadilly Line within the next twenty-four hours. You needn't waste your time tracing this call. Vortex can disappear into thin air faster than Harry Houdini.'

★ ★ ★

Later that day, Peter Hamilton confronted Hermione and Lyle with the latest developments in the case.

'The Piccadilly Line serves Heathrow Airport,' she exclaimed. 'Surely you don't think Vortex would be evil enough to unleash a runaway train on the line?'

Peter's face was ash-grey. 'Vortex has already killed ten people. They're prepared to resort to carnage on a grand scale in a bid to force the government into cancelling its plans to privatize the Tube.'

'Thousands of people could die,' Hermione exclaimed. 'Vortex's latest phone call indicates they've got at least eight members, possibly more.'

Lyle's eyes gleamed. 'You say Vortex rang you this time, Peter? Now that is interesting. Vortex sent you a text message after Norwood Mackintosh's murder. Something must have happened on that one occasion to prevent them from speaking to you directly.'

Peter took a deep breath. 'The Prime Minister has given her personal authorisation for soldiers to be drafted in to boost security on London Underground. A total of four hundred and fifty armed troops have joined the extra police officers patrolling the Tube network.'

'Why don't you switch off the power supply on the Piccadilly Line?' Hermione asked. 'That way Vortex won't be able to unleash a runaway train.'

Peter said irritably, 'London Underground would grind to a complete standstill if we did that every time we receive a terrorist threat. Millions of people would be stranded, and the effect on the city's economy would be devastating.'

'There must be something you can do,' Hermione insisted.

'We've adopted new security measures

to ensure a runaway train doesn't get close enough to a passenger train to cause a collision. The number of trains on the Piccadilly line has been halved. London Underground tickets are being accepted on Heathrow Connect and Heathrow Express rail services. A rail replacement bus service is also operating along the affected route.'

Hermione's memory stirred and she rose impatiently.

'Where are you going?' Lyle asked anxiously.

'There's something I want to check out at Pembroke Grove,' she said. 'I can't believe I didn't think of it sooner.'

'Hermione, Vortex has murdered ten people,' Lyle cried. 'I'm not letting you go anywhere by yourself.'

* * *

Half an hour later, station supervisor Angie Ryder looked up in surprise as Hermione and Lyle entered the control room at Pembroke Grove.

'Hello, Hermione. What are you doing

here?' Darius's voice was filled with concern. 'You're supposed to be taking a few days off to recover from the ordeal of seeing the woman murdered at Westfield Park. You should be off resting.'

Hermione looked at Angie and Darius and thought to herself how much she liked them. The time for subterfuge was over. 'Lyle and I have been hired by Peter Hamilton to investigate the murders on London Underground,' she began briskly.

Angie stared at them. 'Crikey, you had me fooled.'

'I don't believe it.' Darius's voice rose an octave.

'Is Gary Arnott the night-turn station supervisor expected on duty later tonight?' Hermione asked.

Angie nodded. 'He sure is.'

'I hear his wife Jackie is unwell,' Hermione said. 'What exactly is the matter?'

'Gary's wife needs a kidney transplant,' Darius replied. 'Without it she'll die. Here in Britain, close to 6,000 people are on the NHS waiting list for the same operation. The odds of Jackie finding a suitable kidney donor are stacked against her. In America she's got a much greater chance of having a kidney transplant if she pays for it in the private medical healthcare sector. The operation and all the aftercare she's going to need is going to cost Gary a small fortune.'

'I don't wonder Gary looks like a nervous wreck all the time,' Angie said sympathetically. 'I'd feel exactly the same way if one of my family needed a kidney transplant.'

'Gary is beside himself with worry,' Darius said. 'The RMT union has got their hands on a leaked memo from Peter Hamilton. The private companies that are planning to take over London Underground have decided to axe the jobs of all the night-time supervisors. Under privatization, a security guard will look after four or five stations each night. If the British government privatizes London Underground, it's a sure bet Gary will lose his job. He won't be able to pay for Jackie's operation, and she'll die.'

Angie's eyes flashed angrily. 'It's criminal, what London Underground management is planning to foist on their staff and the unsuspecting public. These days, high finance rules everything.'

The door into the adjoining locker room was open, and the silence was punctuated by the muted sound of a ringing mobile. 'Darius, is that your mobile?' Angie asked.

'No, it's Gary's,' Darius replied. 'The key broke off in the padlock on his locker. The fault report centre still hasn't sent anyone here to cut the padlock off for him. He's really annoyed about it because he can't get anything out of his locker.'

The ringing stopped and an eerie silence took its place.

'Angie, I want the honest truth from you,' Hermione said urgently. 'People's lives could depend on it. Who was the station supervisor on duty on Monday evening at five o'clock?'

Angie looked shamefaced. 'According to the staff cover sheets, it was Ashley,' she said. 'But he took an annual leave day at the last minute so he could go to a hypnotist to help him kick his smoking habit. I was supposed to be covering the shift, but I was really attending my niece's baptism.'

'Who stood in for you?' Lyle asked quickly.

'Gary Arnott owed me a favour. He was in charge of the station for the entire shift.'

Hermione felt annoyed with herself for being misled by the staff cover sheets. Valuable time had been lost because of her blunder. 'Darius, who was in the locker room around five o'clock that day?'

Darius replied without hesitation, 'Gary went into the locker room to tidy up his locker. I was in here running the control room. Jacob was downstairs on the gateline — no, wait a minute. That's not strictly true. He came upstairs at five o'clock to get a scarf from his locker. I remember seeing him on the CCTV camera.'

'Did Jacob enter the locker room by the creaking door on the eastbound platform?'

'Aye, that's right, Hermione.'

Hermione turned to Lyle and said, 'Unless I'm mistaken, Gary Arnott was phoning Peter Hamilton to tell him he was the intended victim at Baker Street. Jacob must have walked into the locker room and interrupted the call.'

'It looks as if we've found our man,'

Lyle said. 'But we still don't know if he's the controlling force behind Vortex.'

Hermione suddenly exclaimed, 'Whoever killed Vasilis Demetrious drove his train into Hammersmith station and then disappeared into the night. Gary Arnott doesn't know how to drive a train. That only leaves Jacob.'

Lyle was not so easily convinced. 'Are you forgetting that Daniel Fitzpatrick started off his career as a train driver?' he asked.

'You're right, I *had* forgotten,' Hermione said softly.

The sound of the Westfield Park station supervisor's voice came frantically over the radio console. 'Whiskey Papa One to Alpha One, this is an emergency.'

'Alpha One receiving,' Darius replied. 'State your message.'

'Train 217 has left me on the westbound. It's coming your way in passenger service. You're not going to believe this, but it's being pursued by a runaway train.'

Hermione blanched. 'Vortex threatened to release a runaway train on the Piccadilly Line.'

Lyle cursed. 'It was obviously Vortex's intention to wreak havoc on the West London Line all along.'

★   ★   ★

The driver's voice came urgently over the tannoy of train 217: 'Ladies and gentleman, this is an emergency. We're being chased by a runaway train. If we're hit from behind, the rear carriages of this train will fold up like a concertina. Would everyone in the end carriages please move towards the front of the train by using the interconnecting doors at the end of each carriage. If you don't wanna die, just do as I say.'

The terrified passengers in the half-full train frantically complied with the driver's request. No one noticed the plump middle-aged woman who was sitting in the last carriage by herself. She failed to heed the train driver's message because the tannoy speakers in the last carriage were defective. Ophelia Ogden was already in a state of considerable agitation owing to the phone call she had received a short while ago as she was having supper.

'This is Dr Johnson from St Luke's Hospital. I'm calling on behalf of your sister Rosemary. You're going to have to come to St Luke's hospital straight away if you want to see her before she dies.'

'She was perfectly fine when I visited her this morning. Whatever's the matter with her?'

'A nurse gave Rosemary another patient's medication by mistake. There's been a violent allergic reaction. She can't hold out much longer. She's asking to speak to you one last time. If you don't come to St Luke's Hospital now, she'll be dead the next time you see her.'

Ophelia had lived on her own in a small council flat in Ealing Broadway for the last thirty years. But for the last two weeks she had been house-sitting in Paddington for friends who were away in Barcelona. Within minutes of receiving the phone call, she had donned a mackintosh and head scarf and hurried around the corner to Paddington Central Tube Station. Luckily she just had time to board the train before its doors closed and it pulled out of the station. It was raining heavily and she had the last carriage all to herself.

Ophelia's breath came in short gasps, and she prayed she would reach Rosemary's bedside before she died. The last year had been such a trying one for her sister. First her husband Alfred had died, then she'd fallen over in their marital house at Tooting Wood and had broken her leg. The doctors at St Luke's Hospital had operated and inserted a metal plate. A six-week period of convalescence in a nursing home had come to an end when Rosemary was readmitted to the hospital. Her leg had become infected and the doctors had been forced to remove the metal plate and insert a new one.

Ophelia was so worried about her sister that she failed to notice that the train had suddenly picked up speed after they pulled out of Westfield Park and hurtled along the track without stopping at Pembroke Grove. She was equally oblivious to the fact that the train did not stop at Whitechurch Road, Laburnum Lane, and Shadwell Green. Rain lashed the windows of the train, and the pitch-black night was punctuated by the lights of suburbia flashing past.

Dressed in a London Underground uniform, the killer entered the last carriage. Ophelia's colour was uneven and she was hyperventilating. 'I'm afraid I'm not feeling too well,' she said, staring short-sightedly at the killer's face. 'I'm asthmatic.'

There was a driver's cab at both ends of the train on which they were travelling in order to facilitate a fast arrival and departure from Paddington Central and Tooting Wood Tube Stations.

'There's an asthma inhaler in the first-aid kit in the driver's end cab. Come with me.'

The killer used a J-door key to open the connecting door to the driver's end cab, then gestured for Ophelia to enter the confined space. She was a little unsteady on her feet. Shining through the rear windscreen were the lights of the runaway train that was pursuing them.

Ophelia blinked in the harsh glare. 'My, isn't that train following rather close behind us?' she asked in a puzzled voice.

Suddenly she felt a blow to the back of her head. She collapsed on the floor, where she drifted in and out of unconsciousness.

Laughing out loud, the killer thought, *The stupid cow swallowed my bogus phone call about her sister!*

Less than two minutes later, the silence in the control room at Pembroke Grove was shattered by the startled voice of the station supervisor at Shadwell Green coming over the radio console. 'Sierra Golf One to Alpha One, I've got a one under here at Shadwell Green.'

'Alpha One to last caller, you're breaking up — repeat your message,' Darius rapped authoritatively. 'Repeat your message.'

The station supervisor's voice was shaking. 'I was standing on the westbound platform here at Shadwell Green. Someone pushed a woman who was kicking and screaming out of the end cab of train 217 directly into the path of the runaway train.'

Lyle exchanged startled glances with Hermione.

'Did you see the killer's face?' Darius

317

demanded. 'Can you identify him?'

'No, the light was off in the end cab. It happened so fast. I've got a one under — repeat, one under.'

A feeling of cold dread gripped Hermione and Lyle as they watched Angie Ryder dial 1010 on the auto-phone — the emergency number for the service controller.

18

Jack Perkins sat in the front cab of the runaway train, staring through the windscreen. He was gawping in horror and disbelief. Moments ago someone had thrown a middle-aged woman who was still alive out of the end cab of train 217 into the path of his train. *I must be dreaming,* he thought, but he knew he wasn't. The beam of his headlights had caught her flailing body before she'd disappeared out of sight, then he'd felt a terrible thump — a sure sign of a one under beneath the wheels of his train.

For a brief instant he'd caught sight of the killer's face. The shock was so profound that he let go of the dead man's handle. His train immediately slackened speed. A terrible burning pain seared through his chest. *Christ, don't tell me I'm having a heart attack.*

Cursing out loud, Jack rammed his hand back down on the dead man's handle. The gap between the two trains began to close again. Suddenly his ratchet face was distorted by a grin. *At this rate there's every chance I'll ram train 217 from behind before we reach Tooting Wood*, he thought.

He envisaged the ensuing newspaper headlines. 'Runaway Train on West London Line: Vortex's Night of Carnage.'

Stealing the runaway train couldn't have been easier, he thought triumphantly.

$$\star \quad \star \quad \star$$

Jack Perkins had spent ten minutes waiting at Paddington Central Tube Station before the opportunity he was looking for came along. There were no lights on inside the carriages of train 244 as it berthed alongside platform four — a sure sign that the driver had switched them off because the train had been taken out of passenger service en route to Paddington Central Tube Station.

'What's the matter?' Jack asked as the driver got out of the front cab.

'I had to take this train out of passenger

service at Pembroke Grove. The doors are defective. Are you my relief?'

Jack nodded. He was wearing his old train driver's uniform, so his falsehood went unchallenged. After being fired from London Underground for driving a train under the influence of alcohol, he'd been too lazy to throw his uniform out or sell it on eBay.

'You'll be pleased to know you're running empty back down to Tooting Wood.' The driver walked off in the direction of the staff mess room.

Jack could hardly contain his excitement as he watched train 217 leave platform three. It was destined for Tooting Wood. He strode quickly down the far end of platform four and entered the cab of train 244. There was no sign of the relief driver who was supposed to be taking the train out again. Luck was on his side. Five minutes later, the signal turned green.

Jack guided train 244 out of the station with an ease born of long experience. On the approach to Oakdale Road Tube Station, he employed his specialist knowledge to disable the train's braking system. He then pressed down on the dead man's handle. Train 244 moved forward again. He estimated train 217 was two or three minutes ahead of him further down the track. It wasn't going to take him long to catch up with it because it was in passenger service and obliged to stop at each station along the line.

Now let the carnage and destruction begin, he thought jubilantly.

★   ★   ★

Only one other person knew of Jack Perkins's plans. Like all good ideas, the origins of Vortex had evolved over drinks and a series of talks in a pub with his mate, Gary Arnott, the night-turn supervisor at Pembroke Grove. The last time the two men had seen each other was earlier in the week.

'It's bloody outrageous how you've got terminal lung cancer from the asbestos in the ticket office at Tooting Wood,' Gary growled.

'I wish to God I'd never joined London Underground,' Jack muttered. 'Maureen said the same thing to me before she died.'

Gary said bitterly, 'The station supervisor's office at Pembroke Grove is still quarantined off, waiting for all the asbestos to be removed by the bloody contractors. I'd give anything for the doctors to tell me they were wrong when they said I've only got eighteen months, two years at the most. Emphysema, they say. I wish I'd never joined the sodding company.'

Jack chuckled. 'We've fooled everyone with that electronic voice disguiser of yours.'

'Yep — everyone thinks Vortex is a terrorist group to be reckoned with. The bloody fools. If only they knew we were a couple of lonely old men having drinks in a pub.'

They fell silent, recalling the havoc they had wreaked on London Underground over the last six months. Millions of passengers had had their journeys disrupted. Train services had ground to a halt, owing to the many trackside fires that had been started. There had been mass evacuations on numerous stations after the fire call points were activated. Best of all, the delinquents from the Laburnum Lane estate had done a brilliant job of sabotaging the signalling systems. The lads had been only too happy to oblige in return for the free dope Jack had given them. He'd financed his drug racket by taking out a mortgage on his flat. In all probability, the lads had made a tidy sum selling the dope on.

'That electronic voice disguiser is a useful piece of kit,' Gary cackled. 'My hoax bomb calls have led to numerous station closures. The media have lapped up everything I've told 'em.'

'Have another drink on me,' Jack offered. 'Christ only knows who's pushing everyone under the trains.'

Gazing keenly at his friend, Gary said, 'I thought it might be you.'

Jack shook his head in vigorous denial. 'I reckoned it was you.'

'That sort of thing isn't my style,' Gary insisted. 'I'm determined to bring the government to its knees and stop privatization if it's the last thing I do. But

I draw the line at murdering any one myself.'

'You overstepped yourself this last time, didn't you?' Jack asked. 'What do you think you were doing threatening Peter Hamilton like that?'

Gary shrugged. 'My temper got the better of me, and before I knew it I was promising to let a train loose on the network. It was a daft thing to say, but I couldn't stop myself.'

'Have you been following my advice?' Jack demanded.

'Don't worry; I've got quite a stash of new and unused mobiles in my locker at work. Each mobile gets thrown away after it's been used once. There's no way the police can trace the calls back to me.'

'It was madness ringing Peter Hamilton and threatening him with a runaway train,' Jack said. 'You should have waited until the padlock was cut off your locker and you were able to get your hands on the electronic voice disguiser.'

'I did my best to disguise my voice without it,' Gary said defensively. 'You'd never have known it was me.'

'You were stupid making a threat you can't keep.'

'I thought maybe you could help me out,' Gary suggested.

'Why should I?'

'I lost a twin sister when Maureen died, and you lost a wife.'

Jack considered the matter. 'It would have to be me who helps you out, you useless old woman,' he grumbled.

'Does that mean you'll do it?' Gary asked.

'Yep. I don't see why not.'

Unsure if his friend was being serious or not, Gary added virtuously, 'All I ask is that you don't let a runaway train loose on the West London Line.'

Jack exposed his nicotine-stained teeth in a grin. 'The Heathrow branch of the Piccadilly Line sounds good enough for me. What kind of friend do you take me for?'

* * *

Tooting Wood Tube Station on the West London Line had been evacuated. Acting on the instructions of the service controller, the signaller at Tooting Wood signal cabin had set the points on the westbound track accordingly. Everything was in readiness. It was time to pray for a miracle.

Outside the station, the darkness of the rain-lashed night was pierced by the headlights of the two trains thundering towards their destiny. Only forty yards separated them. In the front cab of the runaway train, Jack Perkins was grinning happily. The operational staff of London Underground were in a catch-22 situation: if they tried to stop him by switching off the traction current in the rails, both trains would grind to a halt and his train would slam into the back of the passenger train. Vortex was on a winning streak tonight.

Jack frowned. The train ahead of him was slowing down. There were now only thirty yards separating the two trains. Suddenly the leading carriage of train 217 veered left onto the Southern Line, the other five carriages arching behind as they followed the thrust of the engine which all at once picked up speed again.

Jack let out a howl of rage. He pressed down on the dead man's handle with all his might. The runaway train shot forward, narrowing the gap between the two trains. Only five yards now separated them.

The next phase of the operation required split-second timing. The signaller at Tooting Wood signal cabin was required to switch the lever on his control panel, thereby resetting the points on the track with immediate effect. It was imperative the runaway train remain on the West London Line instead of following the passenger train onto the Southern Line.

The last carriage of train 217 seemed to take forever to clear the points. Eternity hung in the balance for the operational staff of London Underground.

All at once the passenger train was clear of the West London Line by the narrowest of margins. A strategically placed member of staff acting as a lookout immediately contacted the Tooting Wood signal cabin on an emergency phone line. On receiving the call, the signaller flicked the lever to reset the points. For some inexplicable reason that was not due to human error, they jammed and stayed in the same position.

There was nothing the operational staff could do now to prevent the runaway train from following the passenger train onto the Southern Line. Their best efforts had failed. Disaster was only seconds away . . .

But, incredibly, the momentum of the runaway train was so strong that it broke through the points and continued racing down the West London Line towards the deserted platforms of Tooting Wood station.

A roar of impotent fury erupted from Jack. The passenger train had eluded his empty runaway train. The stabbing pain in his chest returned. In the distance he saw another target — the glow of the evacuated ticket hall of Tooting Wood Tube Station where he had worked in the ticket office with his late wife Maureen.

In the signal cabin at Tooting Wood, the signaller roared down the phone to the service controller, 'The runaway train has smashed through the points on the West London Line. Get the traction current off — now!'

On hearing the message on one phone, the service controller spoke into another: 'Discharge traction current.'

At a top-secret location on London Underground, the request was instantly obeyed by the substation power control room operator. Seconds later, the operator's voice came down the phone line to the service controller: 'The traction current is off.'

Although the electrical current had been withdrawn from the rails, the momentum of the runaway train was so great that it continued to hurtle down the track towards the ticket office at Tooting Wood.

The pain in Jack's chest was excruciating. He let go of the dead man's handle and collapsed in a lifeless heap on the floor of his cab.

Ten seconds later the runaway train hit the buffers of platform two. With an ear-splitting shriek of tearing metal, the front carriage reared up like a metallic monster over the edge of the platform and came to rest on its side in the empty ticket hall. The sound of the crash was heard over a mile away.

Meanwhile, train 217 had safely reached Witton Park station on the Southern Line; and all the passengers, along with Ophelia Ogden's killer, had swarmed out of the station.

Inside the station's C.E.R. room, the COMMS engineer scratched his head and cursed. All the CCTV cameras had been reported as defective half an hour ago, and were likely to remain that way until he discovered what was wrong.

19

Hermione and Lyle woke in a jubilant mood on the morning of Christmas Eve. It was a wonderful feeling knowing that Vortex's reign of terror was over.

'It's ironic that the nation's most feared terrorist cell simply turned out to be a couple of drunks,' Hermione sighed.

'It wasn't for nothing that Vortex boasted its members could disappear into thin air like Harry Houdini,' Lyle said.

Presently, after receiving congratulatory phone calls from DS Nicholas Snare and Sir Roland Anstruther, Hermione and Lyle left their suite hand in hand and walked along the corridor and down the main staircase to the foyer.

Hermione said happily, 'I can't help feeling wonderfully pleased with the part I played in exposing Vortex.'

Lyle's thoughts were still on the warm shower they'd enjoyed together. 'You were absolutely magnificent,' he said loyally.

'If the key hadn't broken off in the padlock on Gary Arnott's locker, we might never have found out the truth. The police got all the evidence they needed last night when they forced open his locker. I've never seen such a horde of mobiles in my life.'

'The police have a lot to thank you for,' Lyle said.

Hermione laughed. 'Gary certainly got the shock of his life when he booked on for duty. The look on his face as he was being arrested was priceless. We now know why Vortex sent Peter a text message after Norwood Mackintosh's murder. Gary was unable to open his locker and get his hands on the electronic voice disguiser. Somehow he must have got hold of another mobile. Gary was lucky no one recognized his voice when he rang Peter Hamilton and threatened to let a train loose on the network.'

'The staff of London Underground did a brilliant job dealing with the runaway train,' Lyle said. 'Jack Perkins was a thoroughly nasty piece of goods. I can't imagine anyone is sorry he's dead.'

Hermione released a sigh. 'I can't help feeling sorry for Darius. It came as a huge shock when he learned his uncle was the driver of the runaway train.'

'Darius is young and resilient. He'll get over the shock sooner than you think. He strikes me as being a thoroughly decent chap.'

Hermione smiled. 'You never believed Vortex was as fearsome as its reputation, did you?'

Lyle shook his head. 'London Underground frequently uses an electronic voice to make tannoy messages on its stations and trains. It occurred to me Vortex might be using an electronic voice disguiser to mask the true identities of their members. Nicholas Snare was saying the police have found a notebook in Jack Perkins's flat. It lists the names of all the delinquents on the Laburnum Lane estate who helped Vortex sabotage the Tube network. Deveril and his team have carried out a series of dawn arrests.'

'Shall we send Deveril a congratulatory Christmas card in a bid to warm the cockles of his heart?' Hermione asked.

'It would be a waste of time,' Lyle joked. 'The man has a heart of stone.'

A blonde woman looked up as he approached the theatre desk. 'Can I help you, sir?'

'I'm looking for Carly Pringle,' Lyle said.

'She's off over the Christmas period. Are you a friend of hers?'

'Yes, I need to speak to her urgently.'

'She came back from Essex this morning. She popped by to get a scarf she left behind on Friday. You've only just missed her.'

'Do you have any idea how I might get hold of her?'

'I'm afraid not.'

As they entered the restaurant for breakfast, Hermione said with a catch in her voice, 'I'd forgotten about Carly Pringle, the last surviving juror. It's a relief to know Jack Perkins and Gary Arnott are no longer in a position to harm her.'

* * *

At Oxford Circus Tube Station, Carly Pringle was standing by the edge of the southbound Bakerloo Line platform waiting for a train. She looked over a customer's shoulder and smiled as she read the *Daily Post*'s front page headline: VORTEX'S REIGN OF TERROR ENDS IN MULTIPLE ARRESTS.

She had good reason to be happy. Her boyfriend Gareth, an officer in the army who had been away for a month on a special overseas mission, was coming home this afternoon. She was looking forward to spending Christmas and Boxing Day with him at his flat in Pimlico. The sound of the approaching train reached her ears.

Suddenly she was pushed from behind. Caught unawares, she lost her balance and pitched forward. The sound of her piercing scream attracted immediate attention. A man wrapped his arms around her and saved her from falling in front of the incoming train. She heard shouts and cries from the public.

'Quickly — someone stop him!'

'What's the matter?'

'Someone tried to snatch this woman's handbag.'

Carly's heart was pounding and she was reeling with shock. People crowded around her, asking if she was all right.

'For a horrible moment I actually thought I was going to fall under the train. Thank goodness this man saved me.'

'You'll be all right, love. Just hang on tighter to your handbag in future.'

'It says in the newspaper there were seven thousand incidents of pickpocketing on the Tube last year. It's disgraceful.'

'This has got nothing to do with Vortex — the police have caught the terrorists responsible for the Tube murders.'

Flattered by the concern of her fellow passengers, Carly decided not to report the incident to the police. There was nothing they could do, since the man had got away. She boarded the train, anxious to continue her day's shopping.

* * *

'If I'd known you were coming, I'd have baked a cake and laced it with arsenic.'

A smile of spurious joviality lifted the corners of Julia Brockman's mouth, and she spoke in a plaintive voice. She was a thin, pale woman who'd obviously once been pretty. An aureole of blonde curls streaked with grey hung around her face, which was etched with lines of suffering.

'Arsenic is a deadly poison, Mrs Brockman,' DI Deveril rapped.

'Only if used in careless quantities,' Julia insisted, cradling a gin and tonic in her hand. 'A little arsenic perks up the complexion. You should try it sometime.'

Flanked by DS Snare, DI Deveril stared at her across the kitchen table. 'I see you've already baked a cake, Mrs Brockman.'

Cocooned in an alcoholic haze, Julia nodded happily. 'A special angel cake for my boy. Today would have been Kevin's twenty-third birthday.'

'We're looking for your husband in connection with the London Underground murders.'

There were footsteps overhead, and Julia glanced up at the ceiling. 'Ashley isn't here. I can't think why you've got your men running around like the Keystone Kops. They won't find him.'

DI Deveril felt his blood pressure rising. 'Then where is he?'

Julia produced a look of wide-eyed innocence. 'I'm sure I don't know where he is. And I don't mind admitting I wouldn't tell you if I did. Not after the way the police arrested our Kevin and sent him to prison for something he didn't do.'

'Mrs Brockman, we've been looking for both you and your husband since Friday.'

'I've been here all that time.' Julia smiled brightly. 'I'm surprised you should doubt my integrity in the matter.'

'You've been gone three days. The Gosfordshire police have made regular checks on the lodge during that time.'

Julia made a tut-tutting sound. 'Call yourself a policeman, do you?' she asked. 'You might have thought to look for me up at the main house. I've been sleeping like a lady of the manor between Lord Milsham's silk sheets. The Elliotts are in the servants' wing, so they wouldn't know, of course. I do hope nothing has happened to my Ashley.'

DI Deveril frowned. 'Why should anything untoward have happened to your husband, Mrs Brockman?'

Julia swayed unsteadily on her feet. 'Well, it's all these nasty murders, isn't it?' she replied. 'The ones on London Underground that you've been telling me about.'

'We think your husband was responsible.'

Julia finished her gin and tonic and put the empty glass down on the sink. Picking up a cloth, she extracted a tray of freshly baked scones from the oven and put them down on the table.

'Currant scones,' she said, sniffing appreciatively. 'Ashley likes them as much as our Kevin.'

DS Snare gestured at the open scrapbook on the end of the kitchen table. 'Is this yours, Mrs Brockman?' he asked.

'It certainly is,' Julia agreed brightly. 'I've been buying all the newspapers and cutting out the photographs of each dead juror. This is my special book of remembrance. It's my way of commemorating Kevin's birthday.' She smiled as memories of her son's past reclaimed her.

As they were speaking, a car pulled up outside. Moments later, Lyle Revel and Hermione Bradbury entered the kitchen and stood some distance behind DI Deveril, who remained unaware of their presence. A tip-off from Mrs Elliott up at the main house had alerted the couple to the fact that Julia had returned to the South Lodge. They were anxious to find out what part, if any, the Brockmans had played in the Tube murders.

'Mrs Brockman, your dead son is a convicted killer,' DI Deveril snarled. 'He doesn't deserve to be remembered — not after the way he killed Tommy Tingwell in cold blood.'

Julia gave an anguished cry of pain. 'No, no — I won't have you talk about our Kevin like that!' she cried in a low, suffocated voice. 'His faults were nothing, absolutely nothing, compared to Ben Skinner's. He was a vile, despicable pig.'

DI Deveril said with a sneer, 'The same is true of your son, isn't it?'

'What would you know about anything? You're a stupid policeman. Our Kevin

341

was falsely convicted of murder because Ben Skinner shot dead that security guard.'

DI Deveril cut her off. 'Mrs Brockman, why don't you make things easy for yourself and admit your husband has been killing the jury?'

'What if Ashley has?' Julia glared at him. 'I certainly won't lament the passing of a single one of them.'

'I think you've been helping your husband.'

Julia smiled vindictively. 'Such a thought never crossed my mind!'

'Both men got what they deserved when they were convicted of Tommy Tingwell's murder,' DI Deveril said brutally. 'The loot from the numerous burglaries committed by Ben Skinner and your son was found at the holiday cottage on the Dorset coast.'

'Ben Skinner rented the cottage from our Kevin,' Julia cried. 'He had no idea Ben Skinner was committing these crimes and hiding the proceeds there.'

There was a tense silence in which she sprinkled some icing sugar on her dead son's birthday cake. 'The jury are nearly

342

all dead,' she gloated.

'There's still one juror left unaccounted for,' DI Deveril said, his eyes hard with suspicion.

'Only another one to go.' Julia laughed softly. 'Is that what you're thinking? An angel cake for my beautiful boy.' She walked over to the sink and poured herself another gin and tonic. She stood with her back to them. There was an air of quiet dignity about her that was strangely compelling. 'As a grieving mother, I'm asking you to leave. I don't want you sharing Kevin's birthday with me.'

DI Deveril cleared his throat. 'Mrs Brockman, I am arresting you on suspicion of murdering the members of the jury that convicted — '

Julia released a bloodcurdling scream. She swung round and lunged at DI Deveril with an eleven-inch breadknife aimed firmly at his chest. He stood frozen on the spot. DS Snare only just pushed his superior out of the way in the nick of time.

Julia Brockman's prolonged howl of rage filled the lodge. Everyone looked on in shock as her face convulsed with fury and the blade of the knife split open a cantaloupe on the kitchen table.

* * *

'I'm sorry to have to ask you to identify your husband's body, Mrs Demetrious,' DS Snare said solicitously.

When Delia Demetrious had first learned of Vasilis's murder, her shock and grief had been so intense it was necessary for her to be sedated. She was now trembling as she viewed her husband's body on a stainless-steel tray in the mortuary.

'It's quite all right,' she said, wiping the tears from her cheeks. 'There's no mistake about it. This is my husband. Vasilis was a good man. He worked hard to provide for me and the children.'

DS Snare cleared his throat. 'Mrs Demetrious, the killer was with your husband when you phoned him on Friday night. Could you please tell me the full extent of your conversation with him?'

Fresh tears welled up in Mrs Demetrious's eyes. 'I rang Vas on his mobile number. He answered it in the front cab of his train just outside Hammersmith. It was his last train journey for the night. I was phoning to remind him to buy the cranberry sauce for our Christmas turkey.'

'What exactly did your husband say, Mrs Demetrious?'

'He said he had a station supervisor from Pembroke Grove with him. They hadn't seen each other for ages and they had a lot of catching up to do.'

DS Snare leaned forward breathlessly. 'Did your husband mention the person's name?'

Mrs Demetrious replied with unwavering certainty, 'Ashley Brockman.'

*   *   *

Later that night, in his office at 55 Broadway, Peter Hamilton smiled at Lyle Revel and said, 'The nightmare of the last week and a half is over. The public can once again travel safely on London Underground.'

Lyle was looking thoughtful. 'You mentioned you'd had some good news regarding Daniel Fitzpatrick?'

'Yes; he handed in his resignation this morning. It was the only sensible thing he could do after his questionable encounter with Fenella at Piccadilly Circus. His reason for resigning, so he says, is because he wishes to sort out his private life. Apparently his wife is divorcing him.'

'It sounds as if she's found out he's been having an affair with another man's wife,' Lyle said.

'The same thought crossed my mind, too.'

Lyle's gaze fell on a copy of the *Evening Herald* lying on the desk in front of him. The front page featured a photograph of each murder victim along with their names: Fenella Lloyd, Oscar Sinclair, Reggie Dalloway, Beryl Livingstone, Elia Toscarelli, Norwood Mackintosh, Liz Gillard, Ulrica Corbett-Jones, Vasilis Demetrious, Jeremy Corbett-Jones, and Ophelia Ogden.

Lyle released a forlorn sigh. It was such a terrible waste of human life. There was a certain satisfaction in knowing that Vortex and its supporters had been arrested. Gary Arnott and the delinquents from the Laburnum Lane estate would be going to prison for a long time. He felt oddly depressed without Hermione by his side. Her parents had returned from Corsica and she was visiting them at their flat in Belgravia.

'What's the matter, Lyle? I thought you'd be a lot happier than you are.'

'Consider the following facts,' Lyle replied. 'Jack Perkins was terminally ill and far too frail to have committed any of the murders. It's a miracle he was able to drive the runaway train. When Gary Arnott phoned you after Ulrica Corbett-Jones's murder, he claimed she screamed like a pig having its throat cut when he threw her off the bridge at Westfield Park. But it would have been impossible for her to scream since she was bound and gagged.'

'Vortex fooled everyone by taking false credit for the murders,' Peter said. 'They always contacted me after the media had broadcast the latest victim's details. DI Deveril is convinced Ashley and Julia Brockman took turns to commit the murders.'

'DS Nicholas Snare rang me a short while ago,' Lyle said gravely. 'It seems the police received a report about a near-miss this morning at Oxford Circus.'

Peter was startled. 'On what line?'

'The southbound Bakerloo. The CCTV footage shows Carly Pringle — the last surviving juror — almost being pushed in front of a train. A customer saved her life. The platform was crowded and the man who attacked her got away.'

Peter looked worried.

'At the time of the incident,' Lyle continued, 'Julia Brockman was under surveillance at the South Lodge pending the arrival of DI Deveril and his men. Her husband Ashley booked into the Cumberland Hotel in London four days ago and went on a drinking binge to blot out the pain of their son's death.'

'Losing someone you love isn't easy,' Peter said quietly. 'DI Deveril was saying Kevin Brockman's body was so badly burned in the prison fire that the authorities identified it by the signet ring he was wearing.'

'Last night Ashley was arrested for

drunken affray and assaulting a police officer,' Lyle said. 'He's been in a police cell all this time.'

'Lyle, what exactly are you saying?'

'Supposing the attack on Carly Pringle was attempted murder — what then, my friend?'

Peter was shocked. 'You surely don't think the killer is still on the loose?'

'That's exactly what I think,' Lyle said grimly.

Once again he glanced at the *Evening Herald*. Suddenly several facts fell into place like the pieces of a jigsaw puzzle.

'My God, I don't believe it.'

'What is it?'

A surge of adrenaline shot through Lyle. He snatched up his mobile and push-dialled DS Nicholas Snare's mobile number.

'Nick, my inner voice has spoken and I finally know who murdered the jury. The truth has been staring at me and everyone else all day from the front of the *Evening Herald*.'

20

Sitting in the carriage of a train, with a hat pulled down over his eyes and a scarf obscuring the lower half of his face, Kevin Brockman looked at the front page of the *Evening Herald* and smiled.

The jury who convicted me are nearly all dead, he gloated. *It's too bad the last juror got away.*

Glancing out of the window, he saw a red signal and shivered. He hated anything that was red, because it reminded him of the day a fuel tanker had run off the road, ploughing into the side of Risely Vale Prison. The fire from the explosion had rampaged through the east wing of the prison, destroying everything in its path. He had been lucky to get out alive. A maintenance bulldozer had been left unattended in the prison yard, and he and the other prisoners had used it to smash a hole in the boundary wall and escape to freedom. Owing to the severity of the fire one of the dead prisoners had been mistakenly identified as Brockman because he was wearing a signet ring he'd won off him in a poker game the previous night. For the last month, Brockman had been hiding out at his dilapidated cottage on the Dorset coast — the scene of his infamous shoot-out with the police. His hair was longer now, and he had grown a beard to hide the lower part of his face.

The train pulled into St James's Park Tube Station. Brockman disembarked and followed the way-out signs. As he passed through the gate-line in the ticket hall, memory reclaimed him.

The day before his arrest, he'd come up to London. He'd been on his way to pass the jewellery to a fence when he'd spotted a couple of policemen on the same train as him. They'd also gotten off at St James's Park Tube Station and followed him up to the ticket hall.

Fearing he was about to be arrested with the proceeds of the robbery on him, Brockman had given the police the slip by darting into the foyer of 55 Broadway and taking the lift upstairs. He had hidden the jewels where he hoped no one would find them. Rather than take the lift back downstairs to the lobby, where possible capture by the police might have awaited him, he had bolted down the fire escape and disappeared into the crowd in the street below.

Brockman now had a sense of his life having come full circle. Unconsciously holding his breath, he pushed open the glass door and entered the foyer of 55 Broadway. A security guard on the far side of the foyer was inspecting several visitors' passes.

Brockman strode over to the bank of lifts and pushed the button to summon a lift. While he was waiting for the lift he looked at the faces of the eleven dead jurors on the front page of the *Evening Herald*. He was glad they were dead.

It was a pity that one of the jurors was still alive. He remembered her well — an attractive girl with long dark hair. His hands unconsciously clenched themselves. There was nothing he'd like more than to strangle the bitch.

*   *   *

Earlier that night, Carly Pringle had dined with her boyfriend Gareth at a restaurant on the Embankment. Her eyes had filled with tears when he asked her to marry him, and she had enthusiastically accepted his proposal. They were now sitting on a Tube train on their way home to his flat in Pimlico, where they planned to finish off the night with a bottle of wine.

Carly held Gareth's hand tightly and beamed happily at everyone she saw in the crowded carriage. As the train pulled into St James's Park Tube Station, she looked out of the windows. One of the passengers had disembarked from the train and was walking past on the platform. Her heart missed a beat.

My God, that looks like Kevin Brockman, she thought. It was hard to tell if it was the same man, because he had a beard and his hair was longer.

Carly leapt from the train onto the platform, seconds before the doors closed behind her. Gareth remained on the train, unable to follow her. She looked through the carriage window and shrugged apologetically at her fiancé as the train departed from the station with him on board. There would be time for explanations later after she returned to the flat.

Her heart was pounding as she followed the man suspected of being Kevin Brockman upstairs to the ticket hall. He was tall and wearing a hat and trench coat, so she was able to keep him in her sights without any difficulty.

She glanced round the ticket hall, which was thronged with customers entering and leaving the station. There was no sign of any police. No one, in fact, was interested in Kevin Brockman or what he was doing.

Carly was expecting to follow Kevin Brockman outside into the street. But he surprised her by entering the foyer of 55 Broadway and darting across to the bank of lifts.

Carly stepped into the lift and quickly turned and stood with her back to him. She couldn't be sure, but she reasonably certain he hadn't noticed her because the other people in the lift were standing between them. The doors closed and the lift ascended.

Her thoughts were reeling. The glimpse she had got of the man before she turned round had convinced her of the fact that he was Kevin Brockman. There could be no mistaking those malevolent eyes.

As long as there are other people in the lift, Carly told herself, *Kevin Brockman is unlikely to notice me.*

The doors opened on the fourth floor and the other people stepped out of the lift, leaving her alone with Tommy Tingwell's convicted killer. Her breathing was shallow and she urged herself to stay calm. She glanced across at the control panel. The button for the tenth floor was lit with an orange glow. Why was Kevin Brockman going there?

By the time the lift reached the tenth floor, Carly had the uneasy feeling that Kevin Brockman was gazing at the back of her head. As the doors of the lift opened, she exited to her left and followed the corridor around a corner where she stopped and listened intently. Brockman made no attempt to come after her. Presumably he had exited the lift to his right. Carly heard the doors close, then the sound of the lift descending. Someone had evidently summoned the lift on one of the floors below.

She exhaled slowly, then counted to five before she returned the way she had come. The corridor was empty.

There was only one place Kevin Brockman could have gone, and that was through a doorway at the far end of the corridor. It led into a dimly lit room.

Puzzled, Carly looked around. Her gaze took in several display boards featuring articles and photographs on the subject of London Underground's history. Kevin Brockman was nowhere to be seen. On the far side of the room, a door was ajar.

Carly stepped through the doorway and found herself on the flagstone roof garden. A light on the wall next to the doorway eerily illuminated the scene. Wooden tables and chairs, interspersed with four large wooden tubs containing topiary, were set out before her.

Brockman was bending over one of the wooden tubs in the far left corner. He was digging frantically in the loose soil for something evidently buried there. All at once he tugged a dark velvet string bag to the surface and gave a satisfied grunt.

The door behind Carly slammed shut in the wind. Her heart leapt nervously and she shivered uncontrollably. Brockman spun round, saw her and froze.

'I'm desperate for a cigarette,' she said in a voice that only contained a mild tremor. 'I followed you out here in the hope you might have a lighter.'

'Sorry — I can't help.' Brockman held the bag out invitingly. 'I expect you'd like to see what I buried in the tub. It's the crown jewels.'

Carly was shocked by his friendliness. For a moment she seriously believed he intended to let her look inside the bag. His smile radiated goodwill. She surprised herself by blurting, 'If those belong to the royal family, I'm handing you over to the police and claiming the reward.'

'I'll come quietly,' Brockman joked. 'There's one thing you can do for me.'

'What's that?' Carly forced herself to return his smile.

'Take your hat off so I can see your face properly,' he snarled, brandishing a flick knife at her.

Carly's eyes widened in shock. She reluctantly obeyed him. The woollen hat slipped from her cold fingers and fell to the ground.

'I know who you are,' he said. 'I saw you at the Old Bailey.'

Carly's teeth were chattering from the cold. 'The Old Bailey? What's that? I've no idea what you're talking about.'

Brockman's cruel laughter sickened her. 'Ben Skinner was a spineless fool. It was easy to coerce him into helping me commit the jewel robbery.'

'I'm sorry, I don't understand.'

'I murdered the security guard Tommy Tingwell.'

Carly gasped involuntarily.

'When the police surrounded my cottage in Dorset, I opened fire on them while Ben was asleep. Later I lied and blamed everything on him in court.'

Carly was unable to keep the shock and outrage out of her voice. 'An innocent man was convicted of murder because of you!' Despite the deep repugnance she felt for him, she was unable to suppress her curiosity. 'Are those the jewels from the Hatton Garden robbery?'

Brockman sniggered like an excitable child. 'There are two hundred and fifty thousand pounds' worth of jewels in this bag. They're my passport to freedom. How does it feel knowing you're the last juror left alive?'

Carly stared at him open-mouthed as memory reclaimed her. 'I almost fell in front of a train at Oxford Circus this morning,' she gasped. 'I thought whoever pushed me was trying to snatch my bag.'

'I went to prison because of you.'

Carly saw the look of animal hatred in his eyes.

'This is where your journey terminates,' Brockman said with a grin. 'It's time for you to join the other jurors in heaven.' The flick knife glinted in the lamplight as he advanced on Carly.

'The police are bound to suspect you killed the jury,' she said in a trembling voice. 'People saw us enter the building together.'

'I don't care. I'm still going to kill you.'

'You never met Ben Skinner's kid sister, did you?' Carly pulled a pistol out of her bag and pointed the muzzle at him.

Brockman stared incredulously at her. 'What are you talking about?'

'I'm Joyceline Skinner.' Carly smiled at him. 'Ben was my brother. He used to call me Jo. We were raised by a succession of foster parents.'

Brockman's expression was a mixture of anger and confusion. 'How the hell did you get onto the jury that tried us both?'

'Our parents died when we were young,' Carly replied. 'Ben gave me the only love I knew as a child. The authorities didn't approve of an eleven-year-old girl and her twelve-year-old brother sleeping together. They split us up and sent us to different foster homes. I was so upset I slashed my wrists. There was no contact between us for years, until I was sent a summons for jury service in the post. I didn't even want to do it. At the Old Bailey I was herded into an assembly room with lots of other people. After waiting three days, my name was called out and I was taken to another room. I almost didn't get onto the jury, but another woman ahead of me got out of doing jury service because she'd booked an overseas holiday. When I saw Ben sitting in the dock, I got the most incredible surprise of my life. He was just as shocked to see me.'

'You're telling me it was as simple as that?'

'Fate had brought Ben and me back together, and I was determined to help him. He would never have committed that robbery if you hadn't coerced him into it.'

'How could you let the jury convict us if he meant so much to you?'

'I did everything I could to persuade the jury that you alone had killed Tommy Tingwell,' Carly said. 'Halfway through the trial I suspected I wasn't going to be able to convince them to acquit Ben of his murder. Each day I followed a different juror home. I'd made up my mind, even then, that I was going to kill them if they convicted him.'

Brockman was astounded. He opened

his mouth to speak, but at first words failed him. 'You killed the jury..?'

Carly smiled and released the safety catch on the pistol. 'Yes. All eleven of them.'

Brockman stared at her. 'I don't believe what I'm hearing.'

'The day the verdict was read out in court was the worst day of my life,' Carly said. 'I consoled myself with the thought that Ben could appeal against the verdict and get a reduced sentence. But his appeal was rejected in February this year. Shortly afterwards, he died in Brixton prison.'

'Ben was too soft for his own good,' Brockman said. 'He cried like a baby when he was found guilty along with me of Tommy Tingwell's murder!'

'I was careful to remain on friendly terms with nearly all the jurors. It made it so much easier for me to keep tabs on them. I could have murdered the jury straight away, but I decided to wait until their memories of the trial had faded. Once the killings had begun, I didn't want them recognizing one another's photographs or names in the newspapers and going to the police before I'd killed every single one of them.'

Carly had expected her luck to run out long before that, but amazingly it had held. After the trial, Reggie Dalloway had helped her to get a job working for Gala Theatre Tickets. At Ophelia Ogden's urging, she had become a fellow member of the G. K. Chesterton Society. Ulrica and Jeremy Corbett-Jones had become firm friends and invited her to be a witness at their registry-office wedding.

'A few years ago I was employed by London Underground as a train driver,' Carly recalled. 'But I soon gave it up because I disliked the shift work. I'd kept my old staff uniform, which made it easy for me to gain access to Vasilis Demetrious's train cab. The stupid fool didn't remember me from the trial. He believed everything I told him about myself. As for Jeremy Corbett-Jones, he was so grief-stricken by Ulrica's death that I didn't have any difficulty persuading him to lay some flowers on the track where she died. Now the two of them are together for all eternity, just like Romeo and Juliet.' Her laughter rose on the cold night air.

'How can you be such a sick, evil bitch?' Brockman asked.

In the soft lamplight, Carly's hair shone like a halo of shimmering evil. 'I was hatched from a serpent's egg,' she mocked him. 'And you can't get more glamourous than that. Think Fabergé.'

'I've got something for you,' Brockman said quietly.

'Vortex did me a favour by claiming responsibility for all the murders,' Carly said. 'I'm going to enjoy killing you, too.'

Brockman felt a frisson of fear. 'I don't know who tried to snatch your bag at Oxford Circus this morning. It wasn't me.'

Carly heard the sincerity in his voice and believed him. London was notorious for muggings.

'I'd like to do a deal with you,' Brockman said. 'In return for my freedom, I'll give you the proceeds from the robbery.'

'I don't do deals with sewer rats.'

Carly was stunned by the sheer force

with which he flung the heavy bag of jewels in her face. White flashes of light danced in front of her eyes. She staggered backwards, her finger tightening on the trigger of the pistol. The bullet sliced through the air, narrowly missing him.

All the hatred and bitterness Brockman felt towards the jury rose up in him. He knocked Carly over the edge of the parapet and sent her plummeting to her death nine storeys below. Her body crashed through the skylight above St James's Park station. Customers waiting on the platform looked up and screamed in horror. She landed face up on the cab roof of the incoming train as pandemonium broke out around her. The faint smile on her dead face suggested she knew she was finally with Ben.

21

Brockman felt an enormous surge of triumph after Carly plunged to her death. The bag of jewels lay on the ground where it had dropped after he had thrown it in her face. Grinning happily, he stuffed it into his pocket.

Above him there was an ominous rumble of thunder, then the heavens opened and the deluge began. He glanced over the parapet and hesitated. It was pitch dark and raining heavily now. The fire escape would be wet and slippery. He couldn't risk taking a fatal fall.

Brockman was gloating to himself as he rode the elevator back down to the ground floor. The doors of the lift opened and he raced across the lobby of 55 Broadway towards the exit.

A uniformed police officer appeared by his side. 'Excuse me, sir, could I have a word?'

From the other side of the lobby,

Hermione and Lyle watched as DS Snare blocked Brockman's attempt to escape and snapped a pair of handcuffs around his wrists.

DI Deveril stepped forward, his eyes gleaming like a cobra's. 'You're not going anywhere, Mr Brockman. You're under arrest.'

★   ★   ★

Presently, after congratulating his security staff on a job well done, Peter Hamilton crossed the lobby to Hermione and Lyle. 'It's been an extraordinary night,' he said.

Hermione turned to Lyle. 'How on earth did you guess Carly was the killer?'

'The truth stared me in the face earlier tonight,' Lyle said triumphantly. 'On the front page of the *Evening Herald*, the name of each successive victim was printed below their photo. The first letter of their Christian names spelled out the message: For Ben Luv Jo. As soon as I saw the message, I remembered Ben Skinner had a sister. After he was caught committing incest with Jo, the authorities split them up. Jo was adopted by a Scottish couple. It's a reasonably well-known fact that the surname of Pringle originates from Roxburghshire in Scotland. Her adoptive name of Joyceline Pringle was printed on the badge she wore for Gala Theatre Tickets, although she preferred to be called Carly.'

Hermione said, 'Uncle Roly is going to be shocked when he discovers she was on the jury. He hates being deceived at the best of times.'

'It probably isn't the first time something like this has happened,' Lyle said. 'Jurors who pervert the cause of justice can expect stiff prison sentences. Ben Skinner wept uncontrollably in the dock on the first day of the trial. I'd say the shock of seeing Jo after all those years was too much for him. By the second day he seemed transformed, as if he'd finally had the confidence to believe he'd win his case. Obviously he was relying on her to get him off.'

Peter said, 'It must have been a bitter pill for Ben Skinner to swallow when the jury returned a guilty verdict.'

'It would have come as even more of a shock if he'd known his sister was going to murder the entire jury,' Lyle said. 'Carly told me she met Reggie on a part-time photography course. It was a lie, of course, because she didn't want anyone to know she'd met him on the jury that had convicted her brother and Kevin Brockman. She also said Reggie had been kindness itself after her brother's death in February this year and had taken her to Egypt to recuperate. She immediately regretted drawing attention to the fact that she had had a brother. In a bid to cover her tracks, she said Reggie had also had a relative like her brother who had died after an oophorectomy had led to post-operative complications.'

'An oophorectomy is an operation to remove one or both of a woman's ovaries,' Hermione interjected. 'Reggie must have alluded to the circumstances of his relative's death without specifying her sex or telling Carly what an oophorectomy is.'

'Precisely,' Lyle said. 'It wasn't until earlier today that I read a magazine article

369

about an oophorectomy and realized Carly had lied to me. There were other lies, too. She claimed she took buses everywhere because the murders had left her too frightened to travel on London Underground. But after she murdered Elia Toscarelli, it was obvious she had travelled to work on the network, because she admitted her journey was delayed by the fatality on the Victoria Line. Carly's warped sense of humour worked to her advantage when she told the train driver, Vasilis Demetrious, that her name was Ashley Brockman. He obviously didn't remember doing jury duty with her. When he spoke to his wife on his mobile, he repeated Carly's lie in good faith because Ashley is also a woman's name.'

Peter smiled admiringly at his friend. 'Lyle and I were shocked when the LUL security rang me tonight to say that Kevin Brockman was on the roof garden. Along with everyone else, we thought he was dead. His encounter with Carly was captured on CCTV. If he hadn't pushed her off the roof, I've no doubt she would have killed him.'

Hermione turned to Lyle. 'My parents are furious with you for getting me involved in another murder investigation. We had the most awful row earlier tonight. It was a relief to get your mobile call urging me to come here. Seeing Kevin Brockman arrested has made my night. You're such a show-off, waiting until Christmas Eve to reveal the identity of the killer.'

'You've never complained about my timing before,' Lyle joked.

Hermione shook her head in wonder. 'I'm still amazed Carly managed to single-handedly kill an entire jury. She must have felt in need of a good holiday.'

'Now she's resting in hell for all eternity,' Lyle said with satisfaction. 'It's strange how some people are unable to let go of the past while others are able to move forward and lead productive lives.'

'I never thought I'd say this,' Hermione said, 'but I actually feel sorry for Ashley and Julia Brockman. It must terrible for them having such an awful son.'

'The Brockmans have suffered enough because of Kevin's criminal actions,'

Peter agreed. 'Now the police know Carly killed the jury, I believe most of the charges against the Brockmans are being dropped.'

'Are you forgetting Julia tried to drive an eleven-inch knife into DI Deveril's chest?' Hermione said.

'Deveril's aftershave has that effect on a lot of women,' Lyle said, his eyes twinkling.

Peter smiled at them. 'I owe you both a huge thank you for all your help. Now if you'll excuse me, the press are waiting to speak to me.'

$$\star \quad \star \quad \star$$

It was New Year's Eve. Hermione and Lyle were among hundreds of people who had come to Somerset House's outdoor ice-skating rink to welcome in the New Year.

'I thought you said Nicholas had agreed to meet us here,' Hermione said.

'That's him now,' Lyle said as their friend skated towards them with an attractive brunette on his arm.

'Is this the same girlfriend as last time?' Hermione asked suspiciously. 'I'm hopeless at remembering.'

'It's Daisy — or Sapphire, I think,' Lyle replied. 'He's had more girlfriends than I've had hot dinners. Being a policeman doesn't always leave him time for a normal social life.'

Nicholas skated to a standstill on the ice and exposed his jagged teeth in a wolfish grin. 'Lyle and Hermione, I'd like you to meet my new girlfriend.'

His companion blinded them with a dazzling smile. 'Hi, I'm Ingrid,' she said in a thick Swedish accent. 'It's lovely meeting you both.'

'You'll never believe what Ingrid does for a living,' Nicholas added. 'Go on, don't be shy. Tell them.'

'I'm an undertaker,' Ingrid explained. 'A lot of people don't believe me when I say what I do for a living.'

Nicholas gazed in awe at the couple performing an exhibition dance on the ice. 'Those two are every bit as fantastic as that ice-skating duo from that television series *Dancing on Ice*.'

'You mean Torvill and Dean,' Ingrid said.

'They *are* Torvill and Dean,' Hermione and Lyle said in unison.

'No way — you're pulling my leg!' Nicholas exclaimed.

Presently, the countdown to midnight began as Big Ben's chimes rang out over London. The crowd erupted with euphoria at the stroke of twelve and began singing 'Auld Lang Syne'. The New Year got off to a dazzling start with the night sky over London exploding into a myriad of beautiful fireworks that lit up such famous sights as the Houses of Parliament and Westminster Abbey. The crowd then took to the ice rink to the sound of John Paul Young singing 'Love is in the Air'. Hermione and Lyle performed their own Torvill and Dean tribute dance with somewhat haphazard results. Afterwards he took her into his arms and kissed her passionately.

'I've come to the conclusion I'd rather endure the occasional inconvenience of murder than live without you,' she sighed. 'It's nice to know our lives have returned to normal again.'

Lyle gazed adoringly into her eyes. 'Here's to a crime-free New Year.'

'It's a wonderful idea,' Hermione said, smiling. 'But in our case, I've got a feeling saying it out loud could be tempting fate.'

We do hope that you have enjoyed reading this large print book.

Did you know that all of our titles are available for purchase?

We publish a wide range of high quality large print books including:
Romances, Mysteries, Classics
General Fiction
Non Fiction and Westerns

Special interest titles available in large print are:
The Little Oxford Dictionary
Music Book, Song Book
Hymn Book, Service Book

Also available from us courtesy of Oxford University Press:
Young Readers' Dictionary
(large print edition)
Young Readers' Thesaurus
(large print edition)

For further information or a free brochure, please contact us at:
Ulverscroft Large Print Books Ltd.,
The Green, Bradgate Road, Anstey,
Leicester, LE7 7FU, England.
Tel: (00 44) **0116 236 4325**
Fax: (00 44) **0116 234 0205**

Other titles in the
Linford Mystery Library:

MOUNTAIN GOLD

Denis Hughes

Rex Brandon, internationally famous geologist, is flying to join a party of prospectors camped overlooking the frozen surface of Great Bear Lake in northern Canada, when his plane is forced down in a storm. Suddenly Brandon faces a 200-mile trek across the frozen wastes. Of the people he meets on his journey — all of whom want to get to Great Bear — several are destined to die, and Brandon cannot be certain that the survivors are who they say they are, or what their true motives may be . . .

WATSON'S LOST DISPATCH BOX

Gary Lovisi

Thomas Jones, a retired professor of English and rare book dealer, is astounded when a young man enters his shop offering an almost pristine copy of *The Strand Magazine* from July 1891, containing the Sherlock Holmes story *A Scandal in Bohemia*. But what shocks Thomas the most is that below the magazine title is a stamped inscription proclaiming in large block letters 'AUTHOR COPY'. Thus begins an astonishing adventure leading to murder — both past and present — and the discovery of Dr. John H. Watson's lost dispatch box!